BANDY'S RESTOLA

BANDY'S RESTOLA

Kimberly White

Purple Couchworks 2011

Published by Purple Couchworks

ISBN 978-0-578-09289-8

This is a work of fiction. Names, characters, places and incidents are either the product of the author's imagination or are used fictitiously, and any resemblance to actual events, locales, or persons, living or dead, is entirely coincidental.

Cover art by the author

ONE

We were an okay family until my brother died. I say this using the yardstick of every family I knew, flesh and blood families here in Wattlesburg, glass and color families on TV. Most other families around here were pretty much like us, on the surface at least. Until Steve was killed, superficial was close enough. Superficial was plenty. No need to dig up from others what you're trying to bury at home. *Okay* infers such a broad range of mediocrity. Exclude the brilliant highs and the desperate lows, and that generic middle ground is *okay*. Digging into it is boring. I'd like to change my name to Pattie O. K. Monk, but I don't think I'm there yet.

Until he died, there was never a reason to measure. In retrospect, it's easy to think so. Revising abstract qualities is easy; it's the tangibles that are difficult. No one wants to know what it's like to be singled out by an extraordinary loss.

I was only sixteen, he was only twenty-one. At sixteen, all I wanted was to be *okay*, invisible to my peers (whoever they were), and mediocre to my teachers. Not to stand out for accolade or ridicule, not to be thought of at all. To avoid the negative attention that brings trouble and demands, to avoid the positive attention that brings expectations and demands. Neither is worth it. And then suddenly, my brother was dead.

And then I was mourning for someone I didn't even know. This is what I knew about my brother: that he died a stupid death, incurred while driving drunk. That he had a certain daredevil streak which I lack. That he was five years older, lived in the same house, shared the same parents and was otherwise a stranger. What did he know about me? That I was a girl and my name was Pattie. The end. Steve craved attention with no fear of reaction, and in boring little Wattlesburg, that naturally included alcohol and a muscle car. Heavy metal fuel and the roving party effect. We will be living with his final effect for the rest of our lives.

Aim to remain invisible. Where he craved action, I feared it. Where he gave no thought to reaction, I was obsessed with it. I would rather have remained invisible than drawn the wrong reaction. Steve's play-hard tactics kept our parents busy enough to be satisfied that they gave enough attention to their children, regardless of the unequal distribution. And that was fine with me. Once he was gone, so was that buffer. I never realized what a tremendous favor this was when he was alive.

We were an okay family... bottom class, just like the rest of Wattlesburg. Our town had been in its death throes for roughly a generation, bled by the economic sands sifting south to Los Angeles and north to Fresno. Our flat-roofed, one-story chipped stucco house was rundown but not quite trashy, same as most other houses around town. Plenty of others were trashier. My father, Raoul, worked off and on in warehouses here and there, and my mother, Doris, worked at the Restola. The Restola was a big rest stop just outside of town, on the other side of I-5. A mecca of delights for the traveler, said the billboard lures posted along the freeway for miles and miles. It was another world over there on that side, and everyone in it passed through the Restola.

There was never a lot of talk in our family about future plans. Existence was plan enough. An established routine was tangible, a plan more akin to fantasy. My life was school, my best friend, Elvia, and home, embellished with romance novels, TV, and revolving daydreams of magically waking up one day as somebody completely different. Someone with real beauty and a real personality, real prospects and real talents. Almost any other face in the mirror but my own. Routine allowed me to live my life without complications, explanations or justifications. School, home, TV, hang out with Elvia, TV, bed. Weekends, a bit more variety - hang out with Elvia, maybe a few others, maybe at the Restola or at the reservoir. Unexpected breaks in routine made me feel like a flounder.

I had acquaintances at school, some I had known for most of my school life, some who were just the latest round of transitory figures that cycled in and out of the school years. Except for Elvia, no one knew me well enough to even know my favorite color. She and I were opposites of the same extreme. Elvia was everything I'm not - beautiful, vivacious, fearless. Her family was pretty much typical for our town as well. Elvia lived visibly, I lived invisibly. I was too mediocre to be popular, however much I professed wanting to be invisible. Elvia could have been as popular as she wanted, but she preferred to dabble in different circles, keeping me as her best friend. For me, it was either a position taken by choice, or a choice taken to justify the position; I was never sure enough to examine it. Not something I liked to spend a lot of time considering, for fear of coming to uncomfortable recognitions. In my fantasies, awake late at night, the popular girls who snubbed me or were snotty to me during the day begged my forgiveness and opened their cliques to me, but I disdained. *No thanks, I would rather remain invisible, where I can look down on you.* Elvia was more secure in her own position of disdain - hers was real, not imposed. She had the requirements, but felt the effort needed to stay on top of the popularity game was better spent on her own self-interests. As long as we'd been friends, I never understood why she chose to keep to the fringes with me, and was afraid to ask or wonder too much about it, for fear that asking the question would cause her to snap out of something and say, *You're right, what am I doing out here with you? See ya.*

Then with the ring of the doorbell one dark early morning, Steve's death shattered everything I had built around myself as completely as if all of Wattlesburg had been bulldozed. Everything was typical, I was invisible, and then, just like that, it wasn't. I wasn't. I was the girl whose brother was dead.

TWO

I dream away
my way back home
another ring of the doorbell and I forget he's dead
run to the door, open to find him standing alone
wearing a police uniform complete with gun and serious face
Of all the things he might have been expected to do
becoming the Law was not one
He says nothing and then he's gone, the house is gone, the town is gone
and I walk a narrow road
red powder dirt trail through the woods
Real woods, deep wild and dense woven
and here I am alone
surveyed by the big beefy trees
Barefoot, the fine red dust coats my feet, cakes my toenails
savage ache and pound of my head in tune with my heart
because I wasn't watching where I was walking and slammed it
on a well-muscled tree arm
Put my hand to my forehead and it comes away bloody
sounds of hissing and slithering lurk behind me
they can't possibly mean me
these aren't snakes that I see
a teeming wall of long fat snakes standing upright on the tips of their tails
like Moses staffs
hop toward me with tongues flickering in and out hissing and menacing
I hold my own staff, I can fight back
swing and slash like a wild woman
scream with the pain in my head escalating blinding staggering fatigue
can't contain a bloody forehead with one hand and swing a staff with the other
without losing my grip on something
In my own hand the staff becomes a snake
squirming to escape my hold

head raised to strike
poison fangs aimed at my hand
scream hurry drop it hurry wake up hurry hurry

Awake the morning of my brother's funeral, lying in bed and not wanting to get up. Not wanting to get up in the worst possible way. Forget that damn dream, I hate snakes, the way they move on invisible legs is hideously creepy. I wished I could go and wash the snakehold-feeling off my hands but there were people out there. I heard chattering voices in the living room and above them all, the dominant voice of my Aunt Lula, my mother's younger sister. Looked at the clock, seven-thirty, the funeral wasn't until eleven. From the rest of the house, I heard a long day coming.

Who else was out there and why were they here so early? Listening closer, I heard two other voices under Lula's. Probably my dad's sister, Bertie, and her dull, overweight daughter, Kendra, here all the way from Fresno by seven-thirty. Where were Mom and Dad? I didn't hear their voices. No reason to get up this early for Bertie and Kendra. Turned over and pretended I was going to go back to sleep. Looked for a place to go in my head until I could. No reason to rush into an ugly day and an experience without precedence in my life. Forget that ugly dream.

Everyone was coming here to comfort my parents for the loss of their son. Wouldn't that save me from having to do it? Right? The bigger the crowd, the easier for me to get lost in it. *Right?* Would anyone see me, would anyone remember my loss? *Oh yeah, he had a sister....* I hoped not. What would people say to me? Nothing, I hoped. What should I say in return? Something wise, I hoped. Like what? Please, don't let anyone talk to me. Above the murmurings of the three women in the living room, Kendra's voice rose, shrill and judgmental. "I can't believe him! How can -"

She was cut off, squelched by a hiss from Lula. The snake dream crept up again. Lula's voice grew louder as she came down the hallway, past my door, past Steve's door. Steve's old door. I sat up, strained to hear as she knocked on my parents' door, soft and considerate, then went inside.

From the crack between the faded pink eyelet curtains, a little streak of sunlight burned across my bedroom ceiling. It was

September and still getting hot. *Isn't this the wrong kind of weather for a funeral? We need weepy, dreary weather to give this whole thing the right perspective.* A tiny spider trekked along the sunlight path on the ceiling, but I was too tired to get up and kill it. *My brother is dead,* I told the spider, who was unaffected by my loss. *My brother is dead,* I told myself. Over and over, practicing, trying on the words with varying tones of grief, looking for what felt right, for a tone that matched the way I felt. Looking for what I thought I should show.

The cop who came to give us the news two nights ago had said, in a sorrowful voice, that alcohol was suspected. I wanted to hug him and tell him not to feel so sorry, it wasn't his fault. He stayed with us until Lula got to the house, sat on the edge of the couch with his head down, almost looked like he was praying for us. I had never seen a cop in our house; the strangeness of that sight was the beginning of this unreal feeling. It was more than alcohol. Steve was always crazy. No one should have been surprised by this. I was so angry that my parents and Lula, even the sorrowful cop, were surprised. Although I had never realized it before that moment, we had all been waiting for this. *Don't pretend now.*

I wondered if someday I would regret that we were never close. Right then, I couldn't see any way that could have been different, there just wasn't anything on him, of him, to grab onto. Did that explain this weird empty sensation I had of being punched in the heart? What could I have done? We lived in different worlds under the same roof.

I turned over on my side, still huddling under the blankets despite the growing heat, searching for a reference point. Who else had a brother who died? Only soap opera people. Someone had a little sister, a long time ago. Someone I barely knew, I couldn't remember their name. No one I knew in school had a dead brother. *My brother is dead.* Trying to imagine explaining it to people, returning to school and going through life with that fact as an irrevocable part of my identity. *Hi, I'm Pattie, and my brother is dead.* Better get used to it. Then I cried for the first time since hearing the news, biting down on the edge of my blanket to keep it inside, telling myself *no no no, not now.*

"This is no time to be lying in bed all day," came Lula's voice, sharp and authoritative, up the hallway and closer to my door. *Bitch,* was my automatic response. Dried my eyes with the sheet while she knocked once and barged in without invitation.

"Time to get up, honey," she said, impatient, reaching to pull the blankets off of me. "Your mom and dad need you up, with them."

"I'm up." My voice was shaky, sitting up and trying to hide my weepy eyes by running my hands through my hair.

She could see that I'd been crying and her tone softened. "You're all they have left, Pattie. They need you to be strong for them right now. Come on, and get up."

"I said I'm up! I'll be out in a minute."

So dismissed, Lula left me alone. Got up and opened the closet door, looked over my wardrobe and wondered how to dress for a brother's death. I didn't have anything black. I wanted to wear something he would have liked, but had no idea what that might be. Showered, then chose a plain blue skirt and short-sleeve white sweater, the plainest thing I had. The doorbell rang again, more relatives coming. Lula came back twice to knock on my door, ask if I was okay in here. Translation: *hurry the hell up.*

Examined my face in the mirror, round face sad and drawn, wished I was anyone else, even someone I would pity under normal circumstances. Automatically, I compared myself to Elvia. My own red-rimmed, frightened eyes versus Elvia's, sparkling and lively, painted with three shades of shadow. My round, doughy features versus Elvia's beautiful face, all sharp lines and perfect skin. My limp, thin hair versus Elvia's cascading black curls, on and on it went. My funeral outfit needed something, so I topped it off with a little gold cross that I never wore, something from my grandmother, long dead. Also dead. It fit, but it didn't. No time to ask why or why not, so I left it on and went out to face my family.

Lula pounced on me as soon as I emerged, grabbed my arm and hissed, "Don't you have anything black to wear? This is your brother's *funeral.*" Without waiting for an answer, she pulled me to the center of the room to be cooed over by the pre-funeral visitors.

The funeral and the burial were too unreal to be happening. Words and faces, roles and places swam and melted into sweaty hugs and handshakes in the nauseating late summer heat. As the rituals unfolded, I wondered how much of it I would remember hours later, years later. Then it was back home for the post-funeral visitors. Relatives, more relatives, friends of the family, people I didn't know but with whom I was forced to share my brother's death. Lula stuck close by and grabbed my arm if I tried to drift away, propelled me in slow motion through the living room to be rewarded by everyone with an opinion of what my grief should be: *Oh honey, you must be **this**, oh honey, you must be **that**.*

It went from unreal to surreal, grief-masked strangers in our living room, crying over someone they didn't know beyond staged family gatherings. Trying to force me to cry with them. *This is my family...?* At most, we saw these people once a year, some far less. This forced superficial closeness only added to my feeling of detachment. I had a sensation of earthlessness, grasping at the air with the ground falling away from my feet. There was something wrong with all of this. This was not the way it should be, however that might be.

Waves of anger, grief, loneliness, resistance overwhelmed me, all fighting one another for dominance. My jaw ached from clenching my teeth and my wake-up headache never did go away. Anger was beginning to win, with a growing urge to violence toward the next person who came near me. Better yet, violence toward Lula. Remembered that ugly dream, lashing out with the staff that turned against me, and I was ashamed of the intensity of my anger at such a time, in such a place.

Lost in all those relatives, Lula still clutching my arm, I had trouble remembering that I was standing in the living room where I grew up. None of this looked familiar, there was no sense of the known in the room, as if I was the out-of-towner. The doorbell rang again, adrenaline shot through my chest. *Is this still a dream? Will that be Steve at the door? This is crazy, shake it off.*

People were holding plates of food and I realized I was hungry. I started to ask for a plate but Lula silenced me with a stony look before I could complete the request. To divert my attention from the food, she steered me to the couch, where my parents were huddled together, plopped me down next to my mother as if I was a toddler. My mother, dressed in black with her hair fresh-dyed and teased to match, took no notice of me. Immersed in her own grief, leaking delicate little sobs into a tissue, she clung to my father's shoulder. He wore a dark blue suit that I'd never seen before, patted my mom's shoulder in stiff, amateur motions, holding his own tears in check behind a stoic expression. It was the last time they were so united.

The visitors took their turns with Mom and Dad, each gave the same canned condolences in low, grieved tones. Once I'd been removed from the midst of the crowd and parked with my parents, no one had anything more to offer me. My parents offered nothing, not even acknowledgment, and seemed to derive no comfort from my presence. I didn't know what I was supposed to be doing, so I sat, wordless and tearless, trying to be invisible while everyone around me played their expected roles. I let my eyes wander the room, trying to recapture that familiarity of place that was missing a minute ago, hearing but not listening to the lowered voices floating in the heavy, hot air. Everyone else in the room looked everywhere but at me.

The room itself seemed ill at ease, unprepared for the gravity of the occasion. I had a clichéd mental picture of funeral gatherings taking place in large vaulted rooms with heavy velvet draperies, while the rain cries outside. *What movie did that come from?* But I couldn't place it. Searching my memory for the movie reference gave me something else on which to concentrate, aside from what was going on around me.

Most of these people had been here before at one time or another, some I had never seen before. Elvia and her parents had been there a little earlier, but I didn't see them now. I couldn't remember another occasion when all of these people were all in the house at once. There were no cousins near my age; at twenty-three, Kendra was the closest, but at that age, seven years might as well have been seventy. She wasn't even likable: she was whiny and thought more of herself than I thought was warranted. There she stood, off to the side, silent and wide-eyed as though she was afraid of being caught enjoying her food, possibly even more uncomfortable than I was.

What time is it? I sat with nothing to say or do and no one to say it to, looking for someone to give me a cue, a clue, anything that felt right, anxious to get the day and its macabre events over with. Lula stood guard over the couch, directing everyone by a nod of her head, a lift of her shoulder, a withering glance (me). My mother continued her low weeping on the couch beside me, still ignoring my presence. As long as I didn't try to move from the couch, I remained invisible.

* * *

By the end of the day, I had been told so many times how I should feel that my mind was reeling, numb and terrified that I felt nothing at all. Whatever my real feelings were, they were lost in this overwhelming bewilderment. *Did I love him? Should I hate him?* What was it going to be like, being a girl whose brother is dead? I was going to hate it, that much I knew.

How was I supposed to feel.... Much later that night, I lay awake, wondering at the ceiling. Lula finally let me eat something after most everyone had gone and it churned in my gut, fighting for precedence in my attention. *What time is it?* Eleven-forty. Outside of my bedroom, the rest of the house was silent. I wondered if my parents were also lying awake. Why should they? They knew how they should feel. Steve was their son. He was my brother. *Was.*

In the living room, Steve's senior portrait sat on an end table that had been moved against the wall and turned into a shrine. I got out of bed and tiptoed from my room to find Lula on the couch, breathing deep under a blanket with her back to the dark room. The surreal atmosphere of the afternoon was gone and the room looked like itself again. Even Lula on the couch was not unusual. She was divorced and had no children, so she spent a lot of time on our couch.

The framed photo was surrounded by funeral flowers, a little statue of the Virgin, a basket filled with condolence cards and a crucifix hanging on the wall above. I don't know where the Virgin and the crucifix came from; I didn't know we had anything like that around the house. I picked up the picture of Steve and sneaked back to my room, turned on the light, and sat up in bed to examine it. We didn't look like brother and sister, not to me. I have our father's round face and fine hair, he had our mother's rectangular face and frizzy hair. We couldn't even claim a link by physical resemblance. The picture was taken three years earlier, when he was a senior in high school. Wearing a tie and a jacket, hair combed down and all flaws airbrushed away, it wasn't really him. But then, how would I know? Our worlds did not intersect. I wondered if he had any notion at the time that he was sitting for his funeral picture. I tried to hear his laugh coming from the studio-posed smile in the picture, but couldn't. *It's your own fault,* I told the picture. *You were stupid and you died.* Had he not died that night, it would have been another night, next week, next month, next year. Didn't they *see* that? At least this way, we didn't have to sit around waiting for it to happen.

Staring at the picture, watching the surface familiarity of his face permute into that of the stranger that he was, I wondered if I was going to miss him. *What* would I miss? The buffer. The diversion. It seemed so impersonal. Already, I saw an unfillable breach, but I was hard pressed to say what had been there before. *Where is he now? Heaven? Hell? Here, watching all of us react to his death? Out in the streets, driving his ghost car in front of semis?* I tried to feel his presence there in my room but felt nothing but the empty warm night, heard nothing but Lula snoring in the other room. What would I expect if he was there? Apology? Regret? Appreciation for being his little sister? Every one of those possibilities was laughable.

In the days and weeks following the funeral, my life continued to feel disjointed and confused. The intrusion of relatives was more upsetting than comforting. When they went home at last, we were left alone with the shamble of our lives. Only Lula remained, because she was the only other one who lived in Wattlesburg. I stayed out of school to be with my parents, trying to be stoic in front of them and Lula, then crying in solitude in my room.

To me, none of the ongoing eulogizing made any sense. Everyone was trying too hard to describe a good boy. Nothing was said about what he really was, a reckless partier who lived a wasted life and died a stupid death. His buddy-buddy friends led their own mourning rituals, away from the family. There were rumors of alcohol-fueled stunts dedicated to my brother's memory, and I was furious - did someone forget to tell these people how he died? It would have been more fitting if they had gone ahead and killed themselves in his memory and gotten it over with.

My parents slipped into a destructive depression in which they turned against each other in vicious blame. Their grief grew and consumed, in two different directions. My father, guilty over having condoned Steve's partying, took his own head dive into the bottle. He made pilgrimages to the reservoir outside of town, where he gathered rocks and laid them out in cryptic symbols, punctuated by empty beer bottles, lit bonfires and drank until he passed out by the fire. He wandered the side of the freeway with bottles of vodka, waving and screaming curses at the big rigs. We knew about this from the cops who kept having to arrest him.

Each time he got thrown in jail, my mother refused to get him out, slamming down the phone sobbing that it was his fault Steve was dead, that it was he who drew Steve into the things that killed him. Rotting in the drunk tank was too good for the unendurable pain he had caused her. Lula sided with her and refused my pleas to pick him up. Each time it happened, I was afraid that this time, they'd keep him locked up. But he always dragged himself back home after a day or two, cradling a fresh bottle.

After a while, the cops got tired of filling out the same report and just dropped him off at home, where he sat in the living room, crying and ranting between pulls on the omnipresent bottle. My mother spent all of her time either in church praying for Steve's soul or at home crying to Lula and me. She refused to let me out of her sight except to go to the bathroom and to sleep. Despite my constant presence, she ignored me, forgot about me until I tried to leave, then clung to me as if I, too, would be killed as soon as I left. She continued to accuse my father of complicity in and responsibility for everything, when she talked to him at all, yet she didn't throw him out of the house. The thought of leaving seemed not to occur to him. Instead of fighting back, he tuned out. Tuned out everyone.

Elvia called and tried to visit after school, but Lula wouldn't let her in, telling her the family needed to be alone. Lula did her best to keep me isolated with them. My parents needed me, she claimed, despite their every indication to the contrary. Lula couldn't be made to see that I needed anyone or anything beyond that, and my parents grew less approachable by the day. My ideal of self-isolated invisibility had come horribly true.

Alone in my room in the middle of the night, I thought about people I didn't see at school anymore. School had just begun, my junior year, before this happened. Not that I missed anyone; I didn't. I didn't miss school or anything about it, except hanging out with Elvia, and it was just strange to be so isolated, to have school removed from my life so suddenly. In a way that I never saw before, school had actually been kind of stimulating. Being around other people gave my imagination something to chew on besides TV characters. Cheerleaders, for instance. I hated them because they knew they were perfect and they had to be sure that everyone else knew it, too. I wished I could look so perfect. I wished I could have gorgeous boyfriends, make everyone adore me. To be popular *if I wanted.* But perfect-looking people are popular even if they don't want it. I could disdain the popularity machine and the savage clique politics and hold myself aloof like Elvia, and everyone would still adore me. Perfection can't help but be worshiped, because it's what everyone wants. But I wouldn't have been so obnoxious about it. I wouldn't have been a cheerleader. Would I...? No, I wouldn't.

And the opposite extreme, the ones who were ugly in a painful way and knew it and were trying even harder to be invisible than I was. The ones everyone pitied. And hated, because you can't help but hate what you pity. The ones who made me glad I wasn't them and you needed that, someone to make you thank God you're you. I thought about them a lot, because in a lot of ways, I was just like them. I was nothing like the ones I looked up to, and everything like the ones on whom I looked down.

Already, their faces were fading, even the ones I saw every day, every year. I wondered what it would be like when I went back. Would anyone remember me? Or would everyone know me because of what happened? Would they say things to me, expecting wise and witty responses, the kind that would not create rumors that I was freaking out? Forgetting was better, but it wasn't up to me.

THREE

After a couple of weeks, I tried to decline going to church, but my mother cried and accused me of abandoning her. So I went, kneeling on the hard bench next to her, uncomfortable and trying not to listen while she mumbled inarticulate pleas to Mary and Jesus. Impatient, I waited in the uncomfortable church as my legs went numb, restless and hating her for dragging me there, hating myself for letting myself be dragged, hating Steve for dying and touching off this whole miserable upheaval. In the cool hushed candlelight of the church, it was easy to forget who really killed him. There was always someone around to tell her that Steve's death was just one more of the All Merciful God's unknowable mysteries.

There was nothing mysterious or unknowable about Steve's death. He got drunk and slammed his car into a semi. What good did it do to pray for Steve now? I imagined myself hurling these words, dripping with bile, at the steely-faced priest who told us to offer our grief up to God. How satisfying that would have felt. I could never do it.

Staring dry-eyed at the crucifix hanging behind the altar, the dead wooden figure inspired no faith or passion in me. So what if Jesus had to die? It was a selfish god who would have someone killed for himself. Now I thought I had an inkling of the grief of the Christians, seeing it in microcosm in my own family. The loss of the only-begotten son. He wasn't a savior, but he was ours. Would my parents' grief have been the same if I had been the one who died? There was no parallel for a dead daughter in my long-ago and forgotten Sunday school teachings. Would I go to hell for having such thoughts in church while kneeling next to my grieving mother?

The carved, bloodless body of Jesus, naked but for a tiny crumpled cloth where his genitals should have been, hovered in state in the forefront of the church. No blood, no guts, death sanitized and sanctified. The statue's hands were clenched in a way that hid the bloody nail holes. One foot, unblemished, covered the other. The head was turned and tilted back so that all you could see of its face was the left ear and underside of the jaw. The Jesus figure appeared to float, untethered, in front of the burnished copper cross. The candlelight shadows wavered across the planes of the cross, adding to the illusion.

Churchgoing had been erratic in our family until then. I guess I had never learned to grieve for Jesus, had never felt anything real about that. Was that why I was unsure of my own grief for Steve? Was I missing something? My mother seemed to be trying to make up for something, but her desperation was futile. Kneeling there in front of the deathless image of Jesus, hiding his face on the cross, all I felt was an intense desire to flee. There was no welcoming feeling of comfort, only disillusionment and distaste. I sort of remembered the Sunday school stories, I remembered being told that God is all-seeing and all-knowing, that God knows what's best for all His children. His children. The priests performed their rituals and preached their mysteries of God's will, nonsensical mythology and a boring afterlife. I think I went into it disillusioned; I don't remember ever buying into much of it, not the kind of belief that raises the dead. *Look at that*, I said in my silent mind to the Jesus figure, *you can't even look at us*. I wondered if I would go to hell for that one, too, but thought it couldn't be much worse than Wattlesburg.

One night the police found my dad wandering down the middle of the freeway, still carrying his bottle, very drunk and calling for Steve. This time, instead of bringing him home, they took him to the county mental facility, sending someone out to the house to tell us where he was.

Lula, my mom and I were playing Parcheesi with the TV on, so that if we talked about anything, it had to be about whatever was coming from the tube. A small porcelain Jesus held court from on top of the TV, holding out tiny glazed hands to bless our worn green and gold livingroom furniture, scuffed-up coffee table and shabby avocado green carpet. Across the room was the shrine to our very own Saint Steven. I snickered at the image this conjured and Lula shot me dead with a frosty look. An anxious look at my mom, then an accusing look at me. If only she knew. Why the hell didn't Lula go to church with her instead of me?

Mom seemed engrossed in herself, detached from the game and from us until it was her turn to roll. Lula chattered about nothing, her artificial voice chipping at my headache. Mom looked like she shared the same headache. Her teased black hair showed a fraction of gray at the roots, something she usually kept hidden under Lady Clairol. Her nails were chewed all the way down and the polish was peeling. Her hands shook and she fumbled with her dice cup the same way she fumbled with her rosary beads. But she perked up whenever a Cal Worthington commercial came on. My mom *loved* Cal Worthington.

I was beginning to chafe under Lula's rule. She had always been around a lot, but she was never a loving or indulgent aunt. Now she seemed to have moved in and that was too much Lula for me. She thought if she could control how we all *breathed,* she could keep my mom from becoming upset. Although the whole family was suffering from Steve's loss, my mother was the only one Lula was interested in protecting.

When the doorbell rang, Mom and I looked at each other, fearful, while Lula pretended not to hear it. When it rang a second time, Lula got up to answer it, to deflect whoever was trying to intrude. Mom started to cry as soon as she saw the cop, biting her lip and sitting up stiff in her chair, clutching her dice cup while the cop described how he eyewitnessed fourteen different trucks almost kill my father before they could catch him.

"That drunken sonovabitch," Lula spat, standing between my mom and the cop, arms folded across her chest. My mom sat silent, staring into her cup and trying to keep her tears hidden from the cop. "Sonovabitch's out every goddamn night partying it up while his family suffers," Lula said, bitter. "You'd think he was the only one who lost a son."

Mom stiffened at Lula's blatant reference. I wouldn't have called what Dad was doing having a party, but I refrained from saying so. I moved to the chair next to my mom, wanting to shield her and support her, but I didn't know how. There was a barrier between us, preventing closer contact.

"It must have been the luck of the drunk that saved him this time," the cop said, in a tone that implied it was our fault for not watching over him. "We almost got ourselves killed chasing him, but we finally got him down. He's not real happy about much of anything right now. We understand about what happened and all, Mrs. Monk, but if we didn't do something with him, he'll just go out and get himself killed the next time, and that won't do anyone any good, will it?"

He gave us a number to call in the morning and left. As soon as he was gone, my mother dropped her dice cup and ran into her bedroom. The door slammed behind her with a sound that jolted through me like a gunshot.

"Now you see," said Lula, wanting to accuse someone of something. But the only one around was me, so she couldn't be any more specific than that.

I was fighting my own tears. Ignoring Lula, wishing she was dead, I ran from the living room, first to my mother's room, but the door was locked. Then to my own room, where I tried to slam the door as hard as Mom did, hoping to send the same kind of shot through Lula. My door didn't have a lock, so I dragged my dresser in front of it. As soon as I did, I had to pee. *Too bad.*

I listened for a slam of the front door, but instead heard Lula go to my mom's locked door, knocking and begging to be let in. "Please, Doris," she wheedled, "you have to let me come in!"

I strained to hear a response, but nothing came. Lula banged again. "Doris? Are you alright? Come on and let me in."

I wanted to scream, but kept it to myself. The hallway floorboard squeaked when she gave up and walked away from my mother's locked and silent door. I waited again for the sound of the front door, instead heard the TV volume rise. *She's not leaving!* I was trapped, inside the house, inside my room, inside my full bladder. Confused and suffocating and overflowing. I managed to wait another thirty minutes before I had to move the dresser and go, which I did as fast as possible, disappearing back into my room before Lula could say anything to me.

I need not have worried about it. She saw me; she chose to ignore me. Fine with both of us.

So tired of sleeping in my tears.... They were not tears for my brother anymore as much as tears for myself and my parents. This time, I recognized that much difference. What would happen now, with my dad locked away and my mom cracking up? Would either of them ever be the same again? As far as my mother appeared to know, her only child was her dead child. I tried to remember what she was like before Steve died, but all I could see was my mother in mourning. It was becoming hard to believe there had ever been a time before

Steve's death. I remembered little snippets, brief moments in history that were doubtless pasted-together wishful remembrances of TV moms, with my own mom's face grafted on. Any mother's smiling face would do, handing me a fresh-baked cookie, asking me how school was today, bandaging a scraped knee with a tender kiss. Little girl stuff with the sweetness of fantasy, nothing of myself past the age of six or so. A life forgotten as soon as it was lived.

guests are everywhere in this glittering mansion palace
where we live, my family and I
rainbow sequins and crisp tuxedos sipping wine from sparkling cut-crystal goblets
Only my brother looks normal, sloppy beer-brand t-shirt and dirty jeans
His dog has died and I'm feeling his grief
it happened suddenly this very morning
and its freshness spills out from him
I'm sorry so sorry my brother
inadequate words
I want to tell him a new puppy is just what he needs but now is not the time
they can get him one tomorrow
but he'll want to choose his own

a blond teenage actress I used to watch
snotty snobbish brat in high heels and an evening gown
trying to tell me the proper way to behave at a palace party such as this
she's beginning to get on my nerves
A sumptuous dinner is announced and she follows me in
Drink, she says, you must drink wine like everyone else
But I'm only sixteen, I'm not allowed to drink
But you have to, it's the law
shove a goblet in my hands and sit down with the adults
bejeweled and hairsprayed and eclipsing me all around
fearful hand clutches my wine
Am I doing something wrong, will I be caught, noticed at all
but no chance of that when a gunman breaks in
shoots a guest in the head
creates screaming chaos
If I can slip in the kitchen to the cordless phone
out the back door to the alley into someone else's back yard

*hide in a grove and call 922 **no** 911*
cower and stare at the phone in my hand
is it adequate will it work am I too far away
will we all be killed
where is the voice
of rescue

FOUR

In the morning, Lula was still here, sitting at our yellow kitchen table reading the paper and sipping coffee. Enraged at the sight of her, I swallowed the sourness rising up from my stomach and opened the refrigerator door to look for something to keep it down.

"Your mom's not in good shape right now," Lula announced without looking up from her paper.

"She hasn't exactly been in good shape since Steve died, in case you haven't noticed," I shot back.

"Now, you watch your tongue, young lady," she said, dropping her paper and giving me a sharp look. "Attitudes like that don't help your mother."

"What attitudes? She doesn't even talk to me, how does she know what my attitudes are?"

"Well, I don't think you should talk to her when you're in this kind of a mood. She doesn't even want to come out of her room, she thinks the whole town is laughing at her and her problems."

"Why would she think that? Nobody laughs at someone whose son was killed!"

"How can you say that? Your dad's behavior is *disgraceful,* has been ever since Steve's death and now he's got himself in the nutbin, where he obviously belongs! No wonder she thinks people are laughing at her."

"Is that what you're telling her?"

"What - how *dare* you!" She was speechless for a second, then found her voice. "You'd better start watching yourself around here, Miss, that's all I got to say. Your mother's entire life has been... been *shattered* and she doesn't need it from you on top of everything else, you hear me?"

"What're you *talking* about, I haven't done anything! I haven't said two words to her since Steve died because she won't talk to me! She doesn't even remember I exist."

"Oh, boo-hoo with your little selfish problems. You don't understand what your mother's going through."

"Yeah? She's the only mother to ever lose a kid. Martin Peterson's little sister was killed and his mother didn't freak out."

"See - that's exactly what I'm talking about. You don't even try to understand your mother's suffering."

"How can I? You just said no one in the whole world could possibly understand, so why should I even try? No one cares about what I'm going through either."

Once again, Lula was wordless for a moment. Mouth agape, she blinked a couple of times, then found her voice. "How can you be so... *cold?*"

"How in hell do you know if I'm cold? You act like everything would be easier if I was dead, too."

She slapped me across the mouth, knocking me off balance and into the refrigerator door. Standing there in shock, I stared at my aunt, who stared me right back down.

"You better start shaping up around here," she said, stabbing at the air in front of my face. "Your mother doesn't need this shit."

"Neither do I," I retorted on my way out the door.

I walked and ran to Elvia's house, twelve blocks away, concentrating on putting one foot in front of the other to keep my tears in check. *I will not cry on the street.* Blind to the other houses I passed, the streets I crossed and the cars that passed by, hoping that would blind everyone to me. It felt strange to be out alone, for the first time since Steve died. Somehow, it didn't feel right. Was I walking okay, or did I look spastic? *Right, left, right... don't trip over that.* What about my arms, were they too stiff? Was I lurching like a dork? My entire body felt out of sync with itself, a dozen different parts jerking in a dozen different directions. I tried to concentrate on relaxing my arms and letting them move in a natural rhythm with my feet, but as soon as I took my focus off my feet, I tripped on a crack and almost fell on my face. Flush with embarrassment, quick look-around for laughing spectators, I hurried on my way. This time, kept my eyes on my feet and let my arms be stiff.

No one was at home at Elvia's house. *Is it a school day?* It hadn't occurred to me. I was starting to feel a little panicky - at the very least, I should know what day it was. The last time I was sure was the funeral. Sitting helpless on the front steps, still trying to keep myself from crying, I prayed that someone would come home soon. *What time is it?* I hadn't noted the time when I got up. *Why do I bother with this? Why don't I just do like Mom and take to my room?* That wouldn't work, Mom had a bathroom and a TV. Lula would be waiting to pounce as soon as I came out to pee or whatever. Now, all I felt was weary, a bone-crushing fatigue had stolen over me unnoticed since the funeral, announcing its full possession of me then and there.

The sun was high in the sky; it must have been around noon. The fall heat hung heavy in the still air, casting an eerie bright silence over the midday neighborhood. I was so sick of the heat. *Doesn't it ever end?* On this treeless street, the worn-out houses were the same as my neighborhood. Same flat tarpaper roofs, same colorless chipped stucco, but for one house painted drastic blue. Just like the one four doors down on our street, except this one looked empty. I hated this miserable town. I'd never realized how much until that very moment. Why couldn't we be from someplace nice? Someplace with a personality, at least. I wasn't sure what that meant, but it sounded good. I tried to picture telling my grandchildren about where I grew up but couldn't think of anything worth telling. Because of this, I would never be able to have grandchildren. How could I, with no stories to tell them about the good old days?

A car turned down the street and I froze, for fear someone would catch me there. *What's my problem? I'm not doing anything.* A dilapidated red sedan cruised by in no particular hurry. I didn't recognize the driver and he didn't look at me. Down the block, a couple of scruffy little kids played a listless game in the chain-link fenced yard of a scruffy little house. The red sedan pulled into the driveway, everyone went inside, and I was alone again.

Why am I sitting here? It could be hours before anyone came home, and it might not be Elvia. I had no idea what I would say to her mother. I didn't want to go back home, and I didn't know where else to go. Was this all there was, stranded and directionless on my best friend's front porch, unable to think beyond this point? It had to change. But to what?

The decision was made for me when Lula pulled up and ordered me into her car. Her voice was loud and she seemed eager to make a public scene, so I went without argument.

We rode home in silence. Lula seemed confident that she had me under control, wearing a self-satisfied look that made me want to laugh and cry at the same time. *I'm losing it.* Turning away to hide my wild grin, I tried to wipe it off before I started giggling. Every bit of me felt pulled tight enough to snap. Watching out the car window, the town looked the same but minutely different, as if everything had shifted one millimeter to the left. I wanted to shake my head and blink to bring it back into focus. *They're going to put me in the nutbin with Dad.*

I almost didn't recognize our house when Lula pulled into the driveway because I was suddenly fascinated by the blue one four doors down. Was our house always this color yellow? Had to be, the paint was peeling. Inside, the same feeling, the way it felt on the day of the funeral. I was an alien. Standing in the familiar/unfamiliar room, near the front door, rubbing my temples, I tried to see the room I had known all my life. It was there but *not there. I don't understand. Has this happened before? I can't remember.*

"Don't disturb your mother," Lula snapped. "I gave her a sleeping pill so she can finally get some good rest."

"Can I have one, too?" I blurted out. "I could use some good rest."

"Don't be stupid," she said, dropping her purse and keys on the couch and heading to the kitchen. I waited for more of an explanation, but she seemed to think that was enough. My head hurt. I massaged my forehead, feeling even more confused, followed Lula into the kitchen.

"What do you mean, don't be stupid? Why can't I have a pill, too?"

"Look," she said, slamming the silverware drawer with a metallic clatter. "We've all had just about enough of your attitudes -"

"We *who?* The only one I ever see is you!"

"Don't make me slap you again, young lady."

"No one *made* you slap me the first time! You're not my mother and you don't live here."

She smiled and folded her arms in triumph. "Well, guess what. Until your mother can handle things again, I *do* live here and I'm in charge. So I guess that just about makes me your mother, doesn't it?"

"In a pig's ass," I muttered on my way out of the kitchen.

"What was that?" she screamed after me, to be answered by the slam of my bedroom door.

FIVE

Where did all this come from? Such a useless thing to wonder. Could this have been predicted? Prevented? How? Did I deserve this? I felt guilty asking that, I should have asked if the family deserved it. I had not realized I loved my brother until he was dead. Objectively, what was there to love? He had paid little attention to me, he was argumentative and crude, and his friends were worse. His friends were more important than we. He wasn't good-looking, he dressed like a slob, like every other guy in town. He was not the kind of brother my friends had crushes on. It wasn't Steve the person I loved, it was more the general idea of *brother*, and that was a bit harder to grasp.

So what. This was not about him anymore. Someone was going to think about me for a change. So what was the *problem*?

The immediate problem was Lula. Or was Lula just a symptom; wasn't my mother the real problem? Had I not grown up hearing her complain about what a no-good son he was, complaints which increased after he left school? Had she come to the same realization, that she didn't know she loved him until he was dead? Maybe that's what all of this church-going was about.

The immediate problem was still Lula. We never liked each other, now my mother was willing to fade away and leave me to her. Being childless, Lula was full of opinions on how I should be raised. With Steve beyond control, most of it had been directed at me.

In a pig's ass.... All I could see ahead of me was Lula's clutch tightening around my throat, cutting off what little air I could gasp. The hot October air in my closed bedroom amplified the feeling of constriction and I felt the weight of the entire house pressing on my chest, crushing the air out of me, the life.... What kind of life did I have here, with a dead brother, a locked-up father, a catatonic mother and Lula?

Here and now... in the sanctity of my room, I saw my future clearly. It was not here. This was not where I really lived; this was only a temporary stopover. Was it time to go? These little-girl trappings were no longer a sanctuary but a hindrance. There was no more life in my Miss Piggy doll, my collection of cutesy porcelain animal figurines, a pennant from my high school. There was much more for me *out there*, waiting. It was the difference between the life of a little girl and the life of a woman, and here I teetered in between, needing just the slightest push to fall into the latter.

The life of a woman requires a job, an apartment, and a car. I had none of those. They couldn't be had in Wattlesburg, not with Lula around. Elvia and I had planned this a thousand times. After high school, get jobs in Los Angeles, an apartment by the beach, wealthy hunks for boyfriends, then husbands, then shopping and lunch every day in fabulous L.A., a city we knew well from TV. We were going to fit right in. Why not start now? Nothing to stop me.

With this mindset, I could shout off all doubts, block out all obstacles. The only thoughts allowed in were how great it would be. *So I'm only sixteen*, but I felt so much older. Recent experiences had aged me beyond other sixteen-year-olds, and the world would be dazzled by my extraordinary maturity. It had to be, it was the only vision I had.

With a burst of speed and urgency, I felt free of my constriction and anxious to be out the door and on my way. But I couldn't just stroll out under Lula's nose, waving cheery bye-byes on my way out. *Kiss my ass, Aunt Lula! Forget to write!* I could sneak out in the early morning, but for the moment, I was free and elated and full of energy, buzzing around the room, pulling things out of drawers, choosing what would go with me to my new life. *Sorry, Miss Piggy.* I had money, over three hundred dollars of babysitting money that I'd been saving for a car. It felt like a fortune, definitely enough to get me there. *There*, that nebulous state of independent womanhood.

My little boombox and tapes filled half of my overnight bag. Toiletries filled most of the rest, so I dumped everything out and started again. I would just buy new things when I got situated. Even so, there was only room for a pair of jeans, some underwear and a few tops.

Start again. Dump everything out again. *What time is it?* Four-thirty. The late afternoon heat hung in the closed room, air thick and stale with memories of wasted girlhood. I didn't want any of it. I was drenched in sweat but didn't want to open the window, for fear of letting my resolve escape with the stale air, for fear of letting Lula in with the fresh air. I would have to carry the boombox; I wasn't leaving home without it. That was fine - one small bag, purse, boombox. That was manageable. The bag was re-packed with my most adult-looking clothes and what little makeup I had. The tapes would have to stay behind. Maybe later Elvia could retrieve them for me, along with the rest of my clothes, send them to me. Better, bring them to me. Maybe. I couldn't see her getting past Lula, though. Lula would think she could force me to come back if she held my things hostage.

Once packed, all I could do was wait, listen to the sounds of the rest of the house while my mind spun out fresh and frantic fantasies of the new life I would be leading over the blaring TV in the living room, the occasional footsteps past my door to the bathroom and back (Lula). Nothing from my mother's room, not even the TV. Scattered sounds from the street, children yelling, cars rolling by, a lawnmower, all of it echoed empty in my anxious soul. There was no life in any of these sounds in this house, in this dying town. Soon I would be free of it all.

After dark, I cracked the bedroom door and peeked into the hall. It was a lot cooler out there. Waiting, listening, trying to figure out where Lula was. All I could hear was the TV, with the dancing TV lights spilling into the hallway. At the other end of the hall was my mother's door, closed against the world with the finality of a tomb.

Closing my door without a sound, I snuck out and into the bathroom, took a shower and collected my toothbrush. Toothpaste and shampoo could be replaced when I got there. I made it back to my room without being bothered, closed the door and felt relief. Now I could open the window and let in the night air. My decision and my preparations made me safe from any intrusion. All I had to do was wait.

I set my alarm for four-thirty AM, got into bed and lay awake, waiting. My mind raced with a million images of what was ahead of me, what kind of job I would find. Something in an office seemed like the most natural place for me. What kind of clothes I would wear: sharp, sexy in an understated way. Distinctive, in a quiet way. Silky and feminine, womanish, in a professional sort of way. I would decorate my apartment near the marina with green hanging plants and pastel velvet pillows on soft chairs and couches. I would have a red Miata. No - a blue Cabriolet. No, definitely the Miata. Elvia would join me as soon as she was able. We would be roommates. But for now, I would have to go it alone. I wouldn't be able to afford a nice apartment like that by myself, not at first. And obviously, the Miata would have to wait a bit, too, but it would come. It had to. It was not going to come here.

Sometime after eleven, the TV went off and I heard Lula pad down the hall, go into Steve's room and close the door. When she didn't come out again, it hit me that she was sleeping in there. In my dead brother's bed. It validated the righteousness of my decision to get out.

When four-thirty came, I jumped out of bed with the excited anticipation of a trip to Disneyland or Hawaii. My hands shook as I dressed and gathered my things and my stomach brimmed with sour acid. I had not eaten since early yesterday and I wondered if I dared sneak into the kitchen for something before I went. No, better wait. I could get something at the bus station. Right now, I just needed to get out of there and on with it.

Would I ever see this room again, the room where I grew up? *Hope not.* Already I felt like a stranger, visiting a museum exhibit, as if the room had withdrawn from me as well. *Goodbye*, I whispered, then slipped out the window and across the lawn to the street, not even bothering to replace the screen behind me.

It was still dark, but with the feeling of transition from night to day. The western edge of the sky, beyond the hills surrounding the reservoir west of town, was showing a dark, rich blue, the beginning of the day. Turning my back on the hills and walking east, the sky was still black and filled with stars. This was a good idea, I told myself, leaving so early. Almost every house I passed was still dark, but for a porch light or kitchen light here and there. There was a feeling of extreme strangeness, different from the strangeness of yesterday, coming home from Elvia's house. Yesterday, everything looked displaced, unfamiliar. Now it just looked old, abandonable. On top of this was my nervous stomach and a sense of doors closing behind me with every hurried step. I fended off my creeping fear of the enormity of what I was doing by filling my mind with the immediate: there goes this street, that landmark, so-and-so's house, out of my life forever. Every memory evoked was quickly shut out, before it could bind me and trip me. *They are not a part of me anymore, I am no longer a part of them, of here, of anywhere.*

There went the storage yard where Eldon Mayfield's carnival lived its off-season, blue corrugated metal sheds surrounded by chain-link fence, topped with curly barbed wire. The yard was piled with pieces of rides, stacked on top of each other, little bitty race cars parked in a line, piles of junk and metal trash, dead midway signs with broken bulbs. Eldon and some of his carnies lived around here, some were born here and would die here, others would never be seen again. I didn't understand the carny people; their hardness scared me. They were the ones who escaped but couldn't stop themselves from coming back. And next to the carny yard, the cemetery, the ones who would never escape.

Walk on... past apathetic power poles stationed along the street, each with dead thistle bushes clustered around the base, tinder-dry in the drought. I couldn't remember ever seeing one of those bushes when it was green and growing. Nothing in this town had ever been green and growing, in my memory. I wanted to set fire to the thistles one by one as I passed them, feel the explosion of fire as it consumed the dead growth all at once, flames roaring and crackling upward, eating up the tar-streaked poles, as dry and receptive as the thistles. But I had no matches. The intensity of feeling evoked by this image was frightening, and blessedly brief. *Shudder and shake it off.* Not that again. I hated that, the sudden arson fantasies that welled up from nowhere and filled me with fire and adrenaline thrill and screaming, frightening intensity.

When I reached the bus station, I was sweating, shaking, and palpitating. Stepping inside the bus station suddenly made the whole idea *real*, and I was gripped with fear that what I was doing was insane. *I'm sixteen and unprepared.* I shoved it aside, refusing to go back now. I couldn't go back and reopen all those doors, suitcase in hand, like a four-year-old fool. *I was pretending I was running away.* Shake it off, I told myself, gather your guts, a woman's life awaits.

The waiting room inside the small bus station was empty, to my disappointment. I had pictured disappearing into a crowd, anonymous, invisible and unfindable. If Lula came after me here, there would be no place to hide. *Don't be stupid, she's not going to come here. How would she know? She'll look at Elvia's and then she'll be stumped.* Elvia didn't know I was doing this, so the trail would be cold. It was a startling thought. I told myself to get a grip on my stomach, then stepped up to the counter and requested a one-way ticket to Los Angeles. My voice cracked and I had to clear my throat and say it again, trying to sound like a woman on important business instead of a runaway teenager.

The ticket clerk was a greasy, skinny guy with dark, stringy hair and a weasely face who looked about forty, despite his acne. He eyeballed me with a look that was too knowing. "Leaving home so soon?" he said, cocking a sarcastic eyebrow at me.

"Huh?" I sputtered, wide-eyed, affronted. *Think fast, try to sound indignant, older,* as if such an idea would never have crossed my mind. "No. Just visiting my cousins."

"Uh-huh. Then you sure you don't want a round-trip?"

"No. I mean, yes, I'm sure." The indignant part was getting easier.

He gave me the ticket with a smirk. I felt my stomach rise again, then turned and marched to the farthest corner of the little room to sit down and wait for my bus. Empty chairs of molded swimming-pool blue plastic stretched out on either side, empty and inviting anyone who might come in to sit by me. The creepy clerk was still eyeing me with that almost-smile and I knew that he knew I was really a runaway. A runaway. It was the first time I'd thought of it that way. *So what.* I tried to reassure myself, but his knowing scared me. Would he call the cops? What would they do to me? *What time is it?* Five minutes to six. The bus didn't leave until seven forty-five. *Hurry up!*

I remembered my empty stomach and walked over to the vending machines. The ticket clerk gave no notice, buried in a newspaper, but I knew he was still watching me. There was a soda machine, snack machine, and some newspaper racks. The Los Angeles Times caught my eye and it occurred to me that I should get one and start checking out the jobs. I'd never had a job before, I had no idea how to go about getting one, and I felt panicked again, but at the same time better with a newspaper in my hand. Surely everything I needed would be in the want ads. My stomach needed something, quick. A sidelong glance at the ticket clerk showed he was engrossed in his paper, inscrutable, but no doubt still watching me.

With a soda, some cookies, and a paper, I sat back down to continue the interminable wait until I could get on the bus. Until I did so, I was still in danger of being found by Lula, despite trying to convince myself that she would not think to look beyond Elvia's. The noise of the newspaper rack got the clerk's attention, and he eyed me sideways, then went back to his own paper. "Don't waste your quarters," he said, turning a page. "No jobs down there for girls like you. They got Ph.D.s flipping burgers down there, if they can find work at all. Only job waiting for you is Hollywood Boulevard hooker, struttin' your little stuff for guys like me." He looked up and gave me a fearsome leer that chilled me to my bones, then dismissed me by going back to his paper.

Isn't there someplace else I can wait? There was the ladies room, but that was too obvious. There was a bench outside, so I went out there to sit, shivering in the fall morning chill while I ate my cookies. I was still used to hot days, so I hadn't thought to bring a jacket. I wasn't expecting cool weather so soon. *What time is it?* Seven o'clock was still forever away. My bag and radio were still inside, stupid me. He could still see me from the window anyway, so I decided to brazen it out and go back inside where it was warm. I didn't care what he thought. That sounded good, but his unsavory assessment of my situation had awakened a nagging fear that maybe I was making a mistake. There was just enough truth in his words to bother me. I'd seen those movies, the TV movies about teenage runaways getting sucked into horrible lives on the boulevard, having to do unthinkable things just to survive, and of course, becoming hopeless junkies in the process. But that wouldn't be me, that couldn't be me, that would never be me. But he took one look at me and saw my plan. What else was true about what he said? *No, no no!* He was just a filthy-minded pervert creep.

The newspaper sat unconcerned on top of my bag, to be read later. I didn't want to give him the satisfaction of being right about me by opening it up in front of him. I just knew the ads were full of things for unskilled sixteen-year-old wannabes - *not wannabe hookers.* Plenty of time to read it on the bus. It was a long ride to L.A.. Too bad I hadn't brought something else to read, to take my mind off the fact that I forgot something so essential as a jacket. What else did I forget? To learn to type, for one. Something I'd always meant to take in school but never got around to. Would I regret it? I would just have to get by without it. *Shoes!* Except for the sneakers on my feet, I forgot shoes. The sneakers wouldn't go with the skirt and blouse I brought for job interviews. How could I be so stupid? There was more money I would have to spend. Three hundred dollars would only go so far. Two hundred and sixty, after the bus ticket. I needed to get a job quick. What else had I forgotten? I didn't want to think about it. *Maybe this is a mistake....* But I wasn't going back, I couldn't go back, I had my ticket, the only way to go was forward.

I finished my cookies and started on my fingers, peeling back the skin from my cuticles until they bled. Told myself to look and act eighteen instead of sixteen, which I accomplished by sitting up straight and tucking my hands in my armpits. It didn't last long, soon my hands were back out and picking at each other. I didn't even have a driver's license. But wait, that was good, I didn't have anything that said I wasn't eighteen. Should I change my name? To what? Where would I stay until I found a job and could get an apartment? Probably a motel. I had no cousins in L.A, no one to take me in. How much would a motel cost?

Nevermind! I was doing this and that was that. Stop being a baby. The ticket clerk finished his paper and got up to refill his coffee, still pretending to ignore me. I was sure he could see everything I was thinking, read every unwelcome doubt I was having. I clamped my arms to my chest to stop chewing my fingers, but that left a void in my concentration that let in more unwelcome thoughts.

Peeling off the front section of the Times, I opened and held it up in front of me so the ticket clerk could see I was not reading the want ads. The only part of a newspaper I had ever read were the Sunday funnies and my horoscope. News and current events didn't interest me; it was only real if it touched me directly.

And now, I would be news. That too had not occurred to me before. They heard at school that my brother died, now they would hear that I ran away. *Did you hear... remember her?* Would anyone but Elvia care? Or had I been out of school long enough to be forgotten? I didn't like the thought of the whisperings that would be going on about me. Well, I was changing all that. Once I stepped on that bus, I could erase Wattlesburg and everyone in it, everything that happened to me, forever. All but Elvia. Already I missed Elvia but that was nothing new, I'd been missing her since Steve died. As soon as I was settled into my new life, I would call her and she could come down when she was ready. It would be great. I could show her around, help her find a job, help her with whatever she needed to get started. I would be *capable*. We had wanted this for so long, fantasized about it all kinds of ways. With these thoughts, I felt like a trailblazer. For a change, I would be the leader, instead of just following along.

SIX

When the bus pulled out of the station, that old sense of unreality added itself to my fear and excitement. What was happening was so extreme that it couldn't be *real*. Even sitting in the station with the ticket in my hand was not as real as this. In the bus station, I was still in Wattlesburg. Now I was moving, being taken, engaged in an incurably forward motion. Would I wake up at any moment, in my own bed, from a dream? I almost hoped so. Would I still get out of bed, gather my things and carry out my plan? *Nevermind!* It was happening, it was for the best. Everything would be fine.

From my window seat, I could see the Restola on the other side of the freeway. The blinking marquee towered over the sprawling complex, proclaiming *Bandy's Restola* in flowing bright neon script, surrounded by flashing blue bulbs, lit up even in daylight. Acres of big rigs in neat lines filled the far end of the parking lot behind campers and station wagons packed with shopping bags, coolers, and clothes baskets, the detritus of families on the move.

Lula worked at the Restola, in the beauty shop. Mom had worked there, too, in the clothing store, before Steve died. The blinking sign winked and waved at me, as if it was telling me I would be back, and it would be waiting.

No. It wasn't possible, I couldn't allow myself to think that. There was no looking behind, only ahead. If I kept saying that, maybe I would believe it. Watching the Restola disappear, blinking *bye-bye* as it went, I felt like the terrified sixteen-year-old that I was. *No.* I was a woman with an action plan. I wondered again if I should change my name, but that seemed too drastic. Every other aspect of my identity had been thrown away, I needed to cling to what little of myself I had left.

The bus passed beyond the town, and I was left staring at the yellow and brown Central Valley, the low hills and the occasional small farm town, each one looking as bereft as the one I had left. *This is not a mistake.* It was time to face the want ads, start working on some kind of real plan. I snuck a look around me, afraid my actions would tell everyone on the bus what I was doing, just like the ticket clerk. The seatbacks were high, so the only other person I could see was a bony old man sitting across the aisle, with iron-gray hair clipped short and leathery brown skin, making painful, methodic smoking motions with a shaking hand. There was no smoking on the bus, so I guess that was how he got by. His blank eyes and sunken face were fixed straight ahead on the seatback in front of him. I could hear low conversational notes floating over the drone of the bus engine, nothing intelligible, but all of it reminding me how alone I was. From the back came a woman's laugh, not an amused, cheery laugh but a bitter, blameful sound.

I decided the old man was not interested in me, and it was okay to get out the want ads. Just opening the paper gave me a sick feeling of how unprepared I was for the adultness of what I was doing. Job hunting. All I knew about job hunting was you look in the want ads, then you go on an interview, and I had no idea what *interview* entailed. They never show job interviews on TV, people get jobs over cocktails or in bed, and I was too young for both.

Shuffling through the sections, looking for the want ads, I bypassed violent headlines, local news, world news, sports, food ads, *where in hell are the want ads?* Pages and pages of nothing but grocery store ads, who cares? Classified ads, *finally.* Employment, page twelve. Jobs Wanted. *Experienced secty seeks position... Welder, exp'd, seeks job....* Maid services, babysitters, handymen, personal assistants. All of these people seeking jobs, each one could claim a title and offer a skill. Jobs Offered! *Here we go.* Accounting, administrative... more titles and more skills I did not possess... mysterious unheard-of titles, ads that made no sense. *What in hell is a clinical perfusionist?* Beauty... *recept/cosmetic sales for upscale skin salon.* Here we go. *Aesthetician preferred.* What? Turn the page.

The ads went on and on, cryptic requirements and offerings whose secret languages were frightening. I was getting that panicky feeling again, the vagueness of my so-called plan becoming more difficult to ignore. I had not considered that I would have to know how to *do* something. I had a simplistic vision of something glamorous and unspecific, with me wearing pretty clothes and dealing with pretty people, driving pretty cars and living in pretty places, just like all the pretty working women on TV. Assuming that whoever hired me would simply teach me all about what to do. Magically waking up one morning (*this morning*) as someone else. The one thing I forgot was that I was not pretty. Suddenly, that felt like a massive handicap. Turning the page, I spot-skimmed for anything that said, *wanted: no experience, no skills, no title, unpretty.*

No jobs down there for girls like you. The greasy ticket clerk's words came back, unwelcome and unsquelchable. What else had he said that was true? *Hollywood Blvd, waiting for guys like me.* I remembered those movies again; it was all too creepy for words. My stomach burbled at an intrusive picture of the ticket clerk handing me some grimy dollar bills on a dangerous street corner and I shuddered, wanting to vomit. I would kill myself first. Shoving it out of my mind and staring out the window, tried to keep my mind blank, focused on beating down my nausea. *That will never happen to me.* Somewhere behind me, a cellophane wrapper tore open, and I wished I had something besides my fingers to chew on.

Los Angeles grew closer and closer, said the passing mileage signs. *What am I supposed to do?* In a few hours, I would be there and would have to get off the bus and – then what? Turning page after page of ads, nothing beckoned through the implicit hostility of prospective employers who wanted everyone but me. *What am I supposed to do?* I wished I knew someone down there, someone I could ask for guidance, someone to meet me at the station and take me home to their house, so I didn't have to be all on my own right away. Someone to give me dinner and a home base and sanctuary. No one. I had $260. I thought I was ready, I thought I was ready. But my prospects were hopeless and I was alone.

I had never realized there was such a thing as being too alone. I thought I was alone at home, but I had no idea. The bleak picture garnered from the newspaper made me want to cry, and I'd thought I was done with that. Adult women don't cry on buses just because things are tough. A tall, potbellied man with a bulbous nose and red eyes staggered down the aisle toward the toilet, grabbing the seat tops for balance and reminding me I couldn't cry on the bus. Again, I choked it back, held my breath and blinked my eyes, staring unseeing out the window. If I cried now, I would hate myself. As the only person left in my life right now, I could ill afford to be hated by anyone. *Everything is under control.* It had to be, there was no other choice. All I could do was not think about it. I could subdue my thoughts, but not the feelings and the strongest one was what a huge, stupid mistake I was making. My body pulled into a tight ball and I stared out the window, eyes trailing on the billowing black smoke of a brush fire on the hills at the distant edge of the valley.

I'll set that fire. I pictured myself up there, on that hilltop, looking down at the faraway string of road crawling with little ant-size cars, wooden matches in my hand. *Mmm*, even better: a fragrant Zippo in my hand. The spring chirps when I open the metal lid, smell the heady fluid. Flick the wheel, sparks, again, this time it catches. Kneel down in the dead yellow grass, touch the flame to the tips and listen while it catches. Extinguish the Zippo by snapping it shut. Watch the firelight grow in the dark early dawn, watch the hungry fire eat and grow, greedy, spreading like a blood stain. Feel the warmth of the fire crackling on my skin. *God! What kind of monster am I?*

The bus started to climb up the Grapevine, and now there were a few trees. They looked as dry as the grass and could flame up just as fast. I wondered what Wattlesburg would look like with trees. It didn't even have a park, just the reservoir behind the hills west of town, where all the underage drinkers, including Elvia and I, go to party. *Went* to party. I tried to distract myself by creating the perfect L.A. boyfriend, but I couldn't make myself believe it.

My search for love in Wattlesburg had been, um, unsuccessful..... I wanted a boyfriend; I couldn't remember a time when I did not. I was in love with the idea of being in love, and there was always a perfect fantasy boyfriend I could steal from TV or from some cheerleader. I used to have no problem being in love with five or six guys at once, including the ones on TV. I juggled different running boyfriend/girlfriend fantasies for each one. Some went on for years, through dozens of versions, from I-wanna-hold-your-hand to actual loss of virginity. It was a lot of work, but it was my passion.

That was another thing. Sex seemed like a great idea in theory, but my physical reality was still struggling with some of the grosser aspects. Sex was great in my fantasies, where I didn't have to do or hear about anything disgusting. On the other hand, my curiosity was growing and my desire was becoming more real. I guess that made me kind of a late bloomer. Elvia was already having sex. More and more people I knew of were having sex, and I was starting to hate being a virgin. But at this point, I still prefered to hear about it second hand from Elvia over doing something about it myself. Desire was still a long way from winning over fear.

Elvia told me all kinds of things, things she said she did and things she said she heard from others. I even believed most of it. It was great fuel for my own fantasies, building on her tales, simply inserting myself into the Elvia role, inserting someone I liked into the guy role. I couldn't always picture myself as wild as Elvia, but I tried. It was just fantasy, nothing I had to live up to.

The boyfriend in theory was not the same as the boyfriend in practice, either. Elvia didn't have a real boyfriend. She went from guy to guy, week to week, and sometimes back again. I would rather have the same boyfriend all the time. Pickings were slim around Wattlesburg. The ones I wanted to go out with didn't want me. The ones who did ask me out didn't quite fit my imagination. Was that just my luck with guys? God, I hated to think I was going to be one of those women who have bad luck with guys. Another depressing thought.

Whenever I went out with a guy, I always seemed to find myself into something way over my head before I even knew it. Always getting hooked into something uncomfortable by someone I didn't even like. Then later, I got to ask myself why I let it happen. I hated not being able to answer my own questions and I hated myself for not being in control.

I could review the chain of events, picking out too many places where I could say, *there,* this is where it started to go wrong, this is where I should have opted out, sparing myself the reproach for having allowed things to slip out of my control. By now, I should know how to control instead of being controlled. Witness what I was doing now, the irony was just sickening. I could create endless situations and conversations in my head where I had complete control, where I had sharp-honed verbal talents that I could only wish for in reality. With my dates, it was rarely a matter of something grossly illegal or sexual, but borderline situations in which I felt uncomfortable and saw the potential for getting into real trouble, should the situation escalate.

Things got real scary the time I went out with Ruben Rios. He was a friend of some guy Elvia was in love with that week, a dropout with his own car and no job. It was a setup date and I disliked him on sight. He began the evening by ridiculing me for being brown but not having a Latino surname. He slammed my attempt to explain that I'm brown because my mother is brown, and she's brown because *her* mother was brown, and her last name was Espinosa. Three generations and the brown hangs on, trying to remind someone of something, it's just that no one can remember what.

Ruben ended the evening by stealing two six-packs from the minimart just three blocks from my house. He was halfway out the door with the beer under his arm before I realized what was happening. I ran out after him, just out of reach of the clerk and we tore out of the parking lot in his Camaro with the clerk screaming, *911's on the way, punks!* I thought both Ruben and the clerk were going to pull out guns and start shooting. Ruben's wild laugh matched my hysterical crying. Stunned by this blatant crime, I was positive we were going to jail and hated myself because Ruben was in no way worth it. I cried so hard that Ruben pulled over and kicked me out of the car, burning rubber as soon as I was out.

In retrospect, Ruben could have been a momentous mistake. Not long after our "date," he was busted for armed robbery and drew three years in prison. I heard about it from his sister, Sharon, who was in my English class. The news rocked me with a jolt that sent me into hiding in my bed for four days. What if Ruben had decided to rob the clerk that night with me, instead of the cooler? What if he had a gun? I could be *dead*. I saw those movies. I was not safe. What if the cops found out about that night and came after me as an accomplice? Would they do that for twelve beers? Suppose they went to my school and asked questions about me, suppose they came here looking for me, told my parents, arrested me. What if the clerk heard about Ruben and remembered us? Elvia's older sister, Maggie, and her husband had both been in jail, and they told us what goes on. And, I saw the movies.

When nothing happened after four days, and I could no longer convince my mother I was sick, I emerged from my darkened bedroom but was afraid to go near a window. Now I see how retreating to the bedroom has a history in our family. My mom was suspicious at first, when I didn't have a fever, but she was convinced I was sick when I wasn't even interested in TV. Nothing happened, I went back to school and never heard another word about Ruben Rios.

For illegal acts, Ruben was as drastic as it got. There was the occasional dope smoker, or the ones who were a little too drunk to be driving. In the back of my mind, there was still a little fear that the Ruben incident would come back to bite me someday.

There was Denny Hoskins, a large and somewhat obese slob. I didn't want to go out with him, but didn't know how to say no when he asked me. I had trouble with that, and I hated it. His idea of a date was to drive up to the reservoir in his brother's trashy van and park. In the back of the van he had a cooler of beer, from which I was glad to drink, to soften his looks and his crude jokes. He pulled me into the back of the van as soon as we parked, pushed me down and jammed his artless mouth on mine. Weakened by the beer, I was nonetheless disgusted by his sudden overpowering insistence. I might not have minded making out with him after several more beers, but now I was in danger of being forced into far more than I intended, drunk or not.

Within seconds, he was trying to force his hand up my blouse. I tried to push him off but he was too heavy, so I squirmed out from under him. *Let's have another beer first*, I said. He mistook that to mean we would drink more, and then have sex. When he kissed me again, too hard and too fast, I panicked and pushed him off. *Fine, you little cocktease bitch*, he screamed, and shoved me out of the van. I lay stunned on the pavement as he sped away, leaving me to walk all the way home from the reservoir in the dark. *It wasn't my fault*, I complained to myself. *Oh no?* I answered back. Lots to hate about myself here. I was too humiliated to call my parents to pick me up and Elvia wasn't old enough to drive yet. It was well after curfew when I got home, still too humiliated to defend myself by telling my parents what happened. I was almost raped, then I was grounded for a month because of Denny Hoskins and boy, was he not worth it. That was when I learned the art of ingress and egress through my bedroom window.

Denny told everyone at school that I had been not only willing, but incredibly nasty in the back of his brother's van. For months, all of his freak friends hounded me and teased me and I had never been so humiliated. Come to think of it, they only stopped when Steve died and I quit going to school. Was that just six weeks ago? Five? You would think that if I was such a slut, his friends would have asked me out, too, but they didn't. I could have said no to them, easy, but I never got the chance. No one "nice" ever asked me out, whether or not it's because of Denny and his asshole friends doesn't matter. It's just my luck with guys.

The droning hum and gentle rocking of the bus reminded me how tired I was, and how little I had slept. The old man across the aisle went into a coughing spasm that sounded as if he was about to cough up everything inside of him, from his lungs down to his feet. Nervous, I tried to watch him without appearing to do so, in case he coughed himself to death right there next to me. No one else was paying any attention to him; in fact, one or two others took the opportunity to add their own coughing to the chorus.

The slow, laboring bus wound up the Grapevine... cars, pickups, even a few RVs whizzed by my window. L.A. drew closer still and I made feeble attempts to tell myself there really was something waiting for me there, where all my fantasies waited to come true. But I knew it wasn't true, it was a mistake, all of this was a mistake. The hills outside my window were brittle-yellow, ready and eager to catch fire, engulf the hills, the freeway, the bus, me. *If only*. I wanted off of the bus, I wanted out of this plan, I wanted off of the planet. Legs pulled up closer to my chest, I sank deeper into the seat, pulled myself backward while moving closer to the end. If I resisted hard enough, could I slow the bus down? Could I find a Twilight Zone where the bus wanders an endless, aimless road and I never have to get off?

If I had pen and paper, I could have made a list of the ways I hated myself at that moment. There was always something jumping out to remind me how together I was not. I hated myself for being on this bus. I hated myself for Ruben and Denny. *This is sick. I get so sick of myself.*

I always liked to tell myself that I didn't mind trying new things as long as it was on a small scale and wouldn't get me into trouble. I liked to fantasize about myself as a tough-talking free spirit, just like Elvia, but I was never able to live up to my own ideal. I envied Elvia's verbal talents and tried to learn from her, but it never translated well from fantasy to reality. Later, I always knew the perfect thing I should have said, when it was too late. Elvia could talk to anyone, she was always funny and confident and always had everyone's attention. But Elvia was beautiful and enjoyed attention and I was just a tongue-tied idiot with too many other faults. That's how it always was, trying to build myself up, tearing myself down again, managing my little self-hatreds like chess pieces, moving, re-arranging and capturing them one at a time to keep them from uniting and taking over the whole board. Always obsessed with what had been spilled to give any thought to what was left standing.

Los Angeles City Limits, said the sign. *Oh, God!* But the bus stayed on the freeway, passing mile after mile of new-looking red tile-roofed bedroom communities crawling up the yellow hills like a scaly rash. Now that I was here, my curiosity was pricked - from the safety of the bus. So many new houses, condos, apartments, shopping centers, there was no end. Nothing like this anywhere near Wattlesburg.

I had envisioned the L.A. I knew from movies and TV: palm trees and picturesque pastel houses, clean tree-trimmed streets, and a highrise downtown. I knew about places like East L.A. and South Central (I saw those movies, too), but these were isolated and contained pockets that never spilled out of their barbed-wire boundaries, weren't they? I would simply avoid places like that. The valley widened, the receding hills were now covered with urban sprawl. I was fascinated, like a caged prisoner. Across the aisle, the hollow old man stared ahead, square hands on his thighs, his head rocking with the movement of the bus.

Still, the bus rolled on. We had been riding through L.A. forever; the sheer size of the city was overwhelming. I had been there once before, on a family trip to Disneyland when I was six, and I didn't remember any of this. Nothing like this. The red-roofed tract homes were gone, now it was tenements and warehouses, an urban ugliness that was not the L.A. of my dreams. This was the *wrong movie*. There's too much blight, no end to it from my filmy, bug-streaked window. The entire city looked like ghetto, uglier by far than any place in Wattlesburg. In the smoggy distance, I saw houses crowding up the hillsides, pitiful refugees escaping the lowland blight for highland smog. The level of voices buzzing around me grew, everyone was waking up and getting ready for the city. This whole thing was a terrible, terrible mistake. My list of things to regret later grew.

SEVEN

The bus station in downtown L.A. made me sick to my stomach with its heady stench of diesel exhaust and urine. Too many people in the bus station looked like perverts and criminals, far worse than the ticket clerk in Wattlesburg. I felt the rancid stares of predators on me as soon as I walked inside. The first thing I needed was a bathroom, which was not immediately evident. A fat old man in dirty, baggy pants and stained t-shirt came toward me, calling, "Miss, oh Miss...."

Restrooms, said a sign way over there. I hurried away, moving as fast as possible without running and drawing attention to myself. I was afraid the ticket clerk in Wattlesburg would report me and the police would be waiting for me when I got there, but maybe he was more anxious to look me up later on the Boulevard.

In the ladies' room, I locked myself into a stall and burst into tears. I choked back the sobs but let the tears flow, sitting with my fists jammed into my eyes, my body shaking with the suppressed sobs. This was too much, this whole thing was too much, too stupid to be believed. *I am an idiot and my life is over.* I was worse than crazy to think I could do this, I belonged in the nutbin with my dad. It was noisy in the restroom, I could go ahead and cry as loud as I needed to and no one would notice. But I couldn't. A staticy P.A. announced bus departures, while outside the restroom door was a noisy commotion that could be either hostile or happy, I couldn't tell. The door flew open and the commotion moved inside, a bunch of girls, with lots of squealing *omigods* over their hair. I was embarrassed for them, I hoped I never sounded like that. Teetering between teenagehood and womanhood, I felt like I belonged to neither age. *What am I supposed to do?* I had no bearings whatsoever. *I gotta get outta here....* My stomach heaved and rolled and I willed myself not to throw up. I didn't want to be seen or heard by those loudmouth girls.

At last, they made a noisy exit and I became aware that there were two people in the stall next to me. Whispered voices, furtive and anxious, one of them male. Holding my breath and frozen to my seat, I listened to the sound of snapping rubber, then a light slapping sound, *thap-thap-thap... thap-thap*, on skin. Then silence, followed by the low aspirated moan of a woman's voice, rising, then cut off, silenced by an edgy sound from the man. *Oh, God!* I was petrified with fear that they would see my feet and my stuff, hear my heart pounding, find me here and then what? Kill me as a witness?

All I knew was that I was trapped. I couldn't get myself to leave, to walk out of the ladies room and face whatever was next for me. It was too big, too much. All of my specious plans came down to this moment, freeze-framed, trapped in a bathroom stall in a bus station as far from the familiar as I could imagine myself to be, as if I had awakened from a coma to find myself there, with no knowledge of how I got there. I wanted to cry again, I wanted to vomit, I wanted to kill myself, but I had no weapon, so I sat, frozen and trying not to breathe, utterly unsure of what to do next.

After a while, the couple in the next stall left and I could breathe again. Now, I noticed how bad the restroom smelled, like years of overflow that no one ever bothered to mop up. I went ahead and vomited, but it just made me feel worse. *What if they're still out there, what if they see me come out and figure I know? What time is it?* The P.A. announced a bus leaving for Las Vegas. More people came in, lingered and left, all of them women, as far as I could tell from my hiding place. Hours went by, what felt like hours, until I was sure enough people had gone in and out that the drug users couldn't possibly pick me out. Could they? I waited a while longer, then collected myself, washed my face without looking in the mirror and snuck out of the restroom to stand in a long line and buy a ticket home from an uninterested overweight woman with tight brown curls and glasses on a chain who didn't even look at me.

I had to spend the night in the bus station, most of it huddled in the bathroom. When I got on the bus early the next morning, I felt a weariness drop over me such as I had never known. I thought I was tired before, but I could have run marathons before this. So I was crawling home in absolute defeat. *So what.* I had no pride left. So I was crawling back to a past with no present and no future. *So what.* I dismissed it all and stared out the bus window, kept my mind blank, seeing nothing that passed by, dozing in and out, setting no fires. Mercifully, my dozing was dreamless.

It was late in the day when I arrived back in Wattlesburg. The tiny, dingy bus station was a welcome contrast to the frenzied, stinking L.A. station. Here, I felt large, adult, in control. There... nevermind. The room was deserted but for the ticket clerk, not the same one from yesterday. *Thank you, God.* Was it only yesterday? It was the first positive note of the whole wretched experience.

Outside, the afternoon was blowing away in the twilight breeze gliding around the building and down the street. The bus pulled out of the station, leaving heavy black fumes behind. Again, I looked around, expecting to see the police or Lula. No one was there. Had they even noticed I was gone? I was crying again as I dialed Elvia's number on the outside payphone.

"Where are you?" Elvia shrieked, with a note of fear I had never heard before. "Your aunt keeps coming over here and accusing us of hiding you."

I almost laughed. Lula didn't think I was capable of thinking past Elvia's house. That gives me a victory that was almost worth the trip. "I'm at the bus station -"

"*What?* Where're you going?"

"No...." I choke on the rest, crying too hard to finish.

"Pattie? Are you there? Are you okay?"

"No...."

"Pattie, what's going on? What're you *doing?*"

"Can - can you come get me please, Elvia? Please!" I was sobbing, overwhelmed by the events and emotions of the last two days, crushed and defeated.

"Don't move, don't worry, we'll be right there," Elvia said, yelling for her mother at the same time. "We're coming, okay? Are you there?"

"Okay." I hung up and sat down to wait, trying to get a grip on my crying before someone saw me. In a few minutes, Elvia and her mother were there. Elvia jumped out of the car before it came to a full stop and I ran, sobbing, into her arms. Her questions came one on top of the other, with no room for answers.

"Where've you *been*, what *happened*, what's going *on!*"

Shaking my head, I was unable to speak. Mrs. Palacio stood by, waiting for Elvia to quiet down before stepping in. "Leave her alone, let's just go home now. You can tell us about it later, Pattie."

We got in the back seat, Elvia holding me and rocking me until we get to her house. I collapsed on their living room couch, feeling as if all of my bones had turned to noodles.

"Are you hurt?" said Mrs. Palacio, calm but concerned.

"No," I shook my head and answered in a tiny voice. How would I ever explain it?

"Everyone's been really worried about you. Your aunt came by looking for you, several times."

"Uh-huh," was my dumb reply.

"Did you have a fight?"

"No - yes." I hated for her to think this was all because of a mere fight, but I didn't want to explain anything, so *yes* was the easiest answer. Mrs. Palacio was such a nice person, with the same pretty face as Elvia but less angular, older and gentler, her eyes more quiet and self-possessed than her wild-eyed daughter. No doubt Lula had been enraged and accusatory, had probably threatened retribution and the law. I could see it in the little worry lines on Mrs. Palacio's forehead. "I don't want to go home, can I just stay here for now, please? Please?"

"Sure," she answered, a little uncertain, already bracing herself for Lula's next onslaught. She took a deep breath. "We were just having dinner when you called. Sit down and eat."

I was guided to a chair and given a plate, which I devoured so fast that I don't even know what I ate and was immediately in danger of throwing it up again. Elvia sat with me the whole time, squirming and watching me eat, dying to flood me with questions. Mrs. Palacio left to go talk to Lula. She was gone for over two hours.

When I finished eating, I felt like crying all over again. I couldn't believe I was there, I had not believed I would be there ever again. For a minute, in that restroom in L.A., I had not believed I would be anywhere ever again. Elvia gave me some Pepto and my stomach felt a little better, which made me want to cry all the more. She was being so careful with me that I thought I must look really, really stomped. I didn't want to talk about any of it, I was too ashamed to have her see how stupid I was. In time, it would all come out, she could wait. We were huddled together on the couch, watching TV when her mother came back, looking wrung-out from what had to have been one hell of a fight.

"I know," I said to poor Mrs. Palacio. "My aunt's a total bitch."

EIGHT

Whatever deal Mrs. Palacio had to strike with my Aunt Satan to let me stay, she did not say. I did not ask questions about my family or the deal, and she did not ask questions about those two missing days.

Mr. Palacio was a truck driver and was only home for a night at a time, every two or three days. He took my presence in stride, teased me about all the hearts I should be breaking out there, just like every time he saw me. He was so different from my own father, who was average height, kind of round, very nondescript. Mr. Palacio was tall and hardbitten, but with a joking personality, shoulder-length black hair, long skinny mustache and ever-present black cowboy hat. The skin of his lean, sharp face hung limp and wrinkled and he drank about the same as my dad. He just never seemed to get drunk. In looks, Elvia is half her mother and half her father; in personality, she's her dad all the way.

Elvia and her mother fussed over me and coddled me, which made me cry again and again. Every time I thought I had cried my last, I was ashamed to find out otherwise, whenever someone was nice to me. *Will I **never** get a grip?* I was so sick of it. Mrs. Palacio told me I was welcome to stay as long as I needed (*sob*), but I knew that sometime, I was going to have to get myself together, whatever that meant, and find some kind of life.

Elvia talked her mother into letting her stay home from school to watch over me and neither of us ever went to school again. We cleaned the house and cooked dinner while Mrs. Palacio worked, and otherwise slept late and watched TV. I watched in silence, unaffected by the emotional swings of the angst and anguish of the soaps and the talk shows, while Elvia maintained a stream of rude commentary.

At night, I had awful dreams about getting off that bus in L.A. and wandering miserable, perilous streets, followed by the fat man from the bus station calling, *Miss, oh Miss...* hiding in roach motels with nothing but a flimsy chain on the door... the face of that smarmy ticket clerk peering in past the weak-looking chain, *see ya down there, babe...* waking up in tears, drenched in the pain of my stupidity, the disintegration of my family, grief for my brother, that touchstone I thought I had buried.

I was so grateful for Elvia, who seemed to know just what I needed and didn't pester me to talk about anything. We left the house as little as possible. She even refused dates to stay home with me. I didn't feel like going out and trying to have fun and I didn't want to run into anyone I knew. I still imagined my problems were the talk of the school, the same way my mother imagined hers to be the talk of the town. School itself felt a million years away. So much had happened since the last time I went to school that I couldn't picture myself back in it without having to start all over again in first grade. As long as we had food in the fridge, it was more fun to stay home. At least I wasn't hiding in my bedroom, like my mother. I tried to get out and change my life. As much of a failure as it was, at least I tried. And, I had escaped Lula and that was all I was trying for.

I pictured my mother still in her room, imagined she had not left it since that awful slam that night, imagined her with her knees nailed to the floor of her closet, so she could pretend it was a confessional, frenzied fingers twisting her rosary and babbling to Jesus until the beads broke and scattered into the corners. Saint Doris the Insane. I wondered if my father was still locked up. I felt worse for him. I didn't blame him for forgetting me; we were both forgotten and pushed out. At least he was trying to deal with it in a human way instead of groveling in a damn church. He tried his best, but it got the best of him and I envied him his freedom to indulge his grief. Thinking of him alone in that hospital, with no visitors made me cry again and again and again. I hated myself for crying; why couldn't I be stronger, why couldn't I be the hard-shelled adult I wanted to be? Or did I blow the one chance I would ever have to grow up?

I waited until a day when Elvia and her mother were out shopping and called the hospital. I had to get out the yellow pages and call about a dozen numbers before I found him. He was still in the detox unit and I was told I could come and visit him on Thursday between one and three. On Thursday, I took the bus to the hospital and held my father's hand for an hour while he cried in silence, his head hanging on his chest, refusing to look at me.

I didn't know what to say to him. I wanted to say, *I love you, Dad, I'm sorry, Dad,* but the words felt so impotent, devoid of real power. Yes, I loved him, but what could he do with that? It was nothing more than a droplet on the immensity of his pain. He was a drunk in a mental hospital. *I'm sorry* is so useless. *I'm sorry* for what? It meant nothing.

Holding my father's limp hand, I wondered if I was wrong to come here. Or, should I have come every day? He knew I was there - he wasn't *that* far gone - and every once in a while he gave my hand a weak squeeze. His uncut, unwashed black hair hung in his face, showing some white that was not there before. He hadn't shaved in a long time. He had lost weight but instead of looking better, his skin hung in florid bags from his wide bones. We were not alone in the room, and that put an extra clamp on my tongue. There was another patient, a thin, heavily tattooed man of indeterminate age with a pockmarked face on a head that was way too big for his body. He sat with his wife, or girlfriend, a young blond woman who looked harried and frightened and randomly familiar.

The man complained nonstop about how full of shit everyone was there. The staff was full of shit, dull and manipulated with ease. The doctors were full of shit, all they wanted was to check the right boxes on the right forms. The other patients, while being full of shit, were so stupid they weren't even worth fucking with, he said. *Wow.* No one here, he kept saying, could touch him for street savvy and pure brains. His big, bony hands fidgeted with the air, his hair, his clothes, arms, each other, never still. His wife/girlfriend had nothing to say but conditioned, monosyllabic responses to his proclamations. She wasn't even looking at him. A big-eyed little boy with a crusty nose, maybe three years old, clung to her leg, squirming as she absently fussed with him.

I couldn't help staring at them. Only the little boy looked back at me; the tattooed man was too self-absorbed and the wife/girlfriend didn't care about anything. An occasional cry of disturbed torment filtered in from behind the dull yellow walls and the heavy institution door with its opaque, wire-reinforced glass window.

Maybe if we were alone, I could have thought of something useful to say to my dad. The tattooed man was sure to include me in his negative assessment, I knew it. I wondered about the woman, what her life was like, how much of it was built around sitting in this room, with that man. She looked resigned to it, blank-faced and dead-eyed, not even a spark of emotion for her little boy.

Visiting hours were over when an attendant came in and removed my father. Another attendant came for the other man, who turned his diatribe on the attendant, fighting verbally but going willingly. He didn't say goodbye to his family. The attendant looked bored and unimpressed. The blonde woman took her little boy by the hand and walked out, unaffected by the visit. I walked out after her and sat on a bench outside of the front entrance, She walked out cool and I had to sit on the bench, biting my forefinger to keep from crying, until I had enough of a grip on myself to walk to the bus stop and get on the bus without embarrassing myself.

A few days later, in the middle of "All My Children," Lula came to the door. Rather than disturb the peace of Elvia's house, I talked to her outside on the porch.

"Your mom wants you to come home," she said, without any preliminary expression of concern or affection.

"How'd she even know I was here? Did she just wake up this morning and notice I wasn't there?"

She looked stunned, flopping a melodramatic hand over her heart. "Now, that's not fair to your poor mother."

"In what way, not fair? I've been here for three weeks and she doesn't even call me. She doesn't care. I could've been anywhere by now." I wished I was.

"Elvia's mother told us you were here, you know that. We thought you needed some space, but *you* haven't even called home to tell your mother a goddamn thing."

She was starting to lose her cool but caught herself. She was on someone else's front porch in someone else's neighborhood. I could think of a thousand things to say to defend myself, but I was stung to silence. Lula has a superior manner that my mother doesn't have. It doesn't invite defiance, and I didn't want to be slapped out there on the porch.

Her tone softened. "You gotta come home, sweetie. Your poor mom's all alone and her heart's broke in a million pieces by everything that's happened. She needs someone to take care of her right now and you're all she has left."

"That's me, the last resort. What're *you* doing?"

"Honey, I gotta go back to work, I got bills to pay and if I don't go back pretty soon I'm gonna get fired, and someone will have to take care of me, too, only I don't have a smart and pretty daughter like you to do it," she said, stroking my hair.

I jerked myself away from her hand, sat down on the steps, buried my face in my hands and cried what I truly and forcefully hoped would be the last tears I ever shed for the rest of my life. The autumn-crisp air stirred to a breeze, scattering a spray of crispy fast-food wrappers down the sidewalk. Steve was the lucky one. I wished I had had a razor blade in that bathroom in L.A. He left me with quite a prize. I had no choice. Lula could pretend to beg, but we both knew I was getting dragged home today whether or not I consented.

Nothing much had changed at home. The Dead Son shrine was still prominent in the living room, Ceramic Jesus was still on top of the TV, and my mother remained locked in her room. At least Lula was gone. I had just begun to get used to the routine at Elvia's house. Without Lula, I could pretty much do at home what I did at Elvia's house, but with no Elvia and no Elvia's parents. The TV in my mom's room blared twenty-four hours a day and I took to sleeping on the couch with the living room TV on to drown it out. Elvia and I still watched our shows together over the phone, and sometimes she even came over. Lula dropped in whenever she wanted, and she sent Elvia home if she found her there. I cleaned the house, watched TV and read until four in the morning, eating whatever odds and ends I found in the kitchen, never preparing a meal in the fundamental sense and almost never seeing my mother. The door to Steve's room was closed, and I stayed out. The room seemed doubly contaminated, with Steve being dead and Lula having slept there. Lula brought groceries, did a brief check on my mom, made sure I was still there and then was gone, apparently tired of her role as caretaker.

When I first came home, I tried to get my mother to either come out or let me in. She either ignored me or snapped off the TV, promising me in a weepy voice through the door that I could come in later, after she'd had a little rest. The TV went back on, later never came and after a while, I gave up. She came out to eat when she thought I was asleep. Sometimes she came into the living room and stood over me, watching me pretend to sleep. I don't know why I pretended, why I couldn't just open my eyes and talk to her. It felt like it would be unfair, kind of like an ambush. In the moment, when she was standing there, I didn't know what I would say anyway. I had nothing that would make her feel better. Then she went back to her room to cry herself to sleep to the lullaby of the TV, the intermittent blasting of *Go-see-Cal, go-see-Cal, go-see-Cal* that saturated late night TV.

My mother had always been in love with Cal Worthington, the used-car king of California. I guess Cal is the one thing that was still there for her, unchanged. Cal was the best-looking man she had ever seen, with his wavy gray hair, his laugh lines and his western clothes, always promising to take better care of you than anyone else. Always begging you to come see him, *go-see-Cal, save-me-Cal, love-me-Cal, go-see-Cal, go-see-Cal, go-see-Cal.* Divine Cal. She would have done better praying to him.

NINE

We lived on cupcakes and potato chips and other foil-wrapped prep-free foods provided by Lula. That was how she ate at her house; that was why she was divorced. I lived in sweats and pajamas, wearing the same cocoon-like outfit every day until it got too ripe, then switched it out for more of the same. It was boring and depressing. I thought about going back to Elvia's house, but Lula wouldn't let me get away with that a second time. She made that promise (threat) to me several times. Her visits were brief; as long as she found me at home, she was satisfied.

I wasn't a hundred percent sure my mother was even in her room anymore. Maybe I'd been sleeping better, but I hadn't seen her come out in the middle of the night for a while. I tried keeping track of the food quantities to see if she still ate, but I lost track and gave up. For all anyone knew, she was the one who skipped to L.A. Gone to see Cal. The TV in her room still ran nonstop, drowning out any possible sound of life in there. Once in a while I tried to talk to her but the door remained locked and she ignored my pleas to open it. Once in a while I heard the toilet flush, and that made me feel better. I worried about her, but I was too timid to force my way in. Is it right to break down your mother's door, just because she won't talk to you? At least I made an effort to let her know I was here, and that's more than she was doing for me.

Then one day, my father came home. At first, I was happy, believing he had come home because he was cured. Now, I could look to him to bestow his brand new mental health on his family and make things as whole as possible again. However.... He lost no time in proving he was in no way *cured*. He came home with a fresh bottle in his arms, like a new baby he was bringing home from the hospital. Instead of finding redemption, I was now captive to two completely dysfunctional human beings. When he found his bedroom door locked and my mom refusing to answer his knock, he sat down on the floor and cried, with the same abandonment of hope I'd seen in the hospital.

That was it for me, too. Something had to happen before I turned into a mumbling catatonic like them. Even school would be better than this. I helped myself to my mother's car keys and drove to the Restola, where Lula was at work in the beauty salon, then waited impatiently while she finished frosting a puffy-faced woman with a mean expression. When she was done, I demanded that she come home with me, *now*. The look in my eyes must have scared her, because she followed me without question or argument.

Together, Lula and I forced open my mother's door and went inside. *Go-see-Cal, go-see-Cal, go-see-Cal,* sang the tinny voice of the TV in the dark room. Flannel blankets were hung over the windows and the air was alive with dust motes, swimming free in the flickering dead-blue light of the TV. My mother lay on the bed, her head propped forward with pillows and her bloodshot eyes fixed on the tube. *I will stand upon my head to beat all deals....* Her long black hair was fantastically matted and showing a wide strip of gray roots and her face was skeletal. Maybe I should have paid more attention while counting the cupcakes and done this a long time ago. Crumpled photos littered the bedspread and the dusty air was heavy and unused, as though she had dispensed with breathing altogether. The tomblike feel of the room gave me the creeps and a touch of claustrophobia. There was a momentary sensation of my own death, entombed, crumbling and forgotten. Lula turned off the TV with a violent jerk. The TV voice died with a perturbed crackle and for a split second, the silence was time-stopping. My mother's eyes blinked, but remained fixed on the blank screen. She looked like a very old woman, and Lula and I stared at her with our mouths open. Lula recovered first and turned on me, shoving me out of the room, past my dad, who was still sitting in the hall.

"*What happened?* You were supposed to be taking care of her - is this what you call *taking care* of someone?" She went into my mother's room and slammed the door in my face, leaving me standing in the hall with my jaw on the ground, astonished at her unexpected attack. My father gave me a pitying look. It was another good time to flee to Elvia's.

A couple of days later, Lula came to get me again, bringing me home with the threat of the police if I didn't come and if I ever tried to leave again. Meekly I went, hating myself for not having the balls to call her bluff and take the police instead. When we got home, my mother was sitting in the living room, newly coifed and made-up, with my father, freshly shaved, cut and combed. Mom clutched a cigarette and Dad clutched a beer. Both wore such fragile expressions that I almost wished they would go catatonic again. They looked like dollhouse parents in their stiff poses, ready to topple over if anyone breathed.

Lula stayed for another week, just long enough to ensure that everyone knew their proper poses, guiding everyone's actions into a routine to which we would be able to adhere without cracking our masks.

My dad was the first to begin to return to life and shake Lula's control. Bravely, he tried to find a new state of normalcy, while still struggling with the fact that nothing was the same as before. Having lost his warehouse job when his drinking went out of control, he took odd jobs where he could find them. Jobs were few in a depressed town like ours, where you worked at the Restola, at the warehouses, way out of town, or not at all. He still drank a lot, but he got out of the house every day. At home he was quietly incoherent, moving like a ghost through the house from chair to refrigerator to bathroom to bedroom, out of everyone else's way.

I mourned what died in my father with Steve: his jolliness and his indulgence, his comedic fumbling which was now pathetic mumbling. Lula dragged my mother out of the house more and more, and at last she felt restored enough to go back to work at the Restola. Slowly, Lula's clamps on my movements loosened and it felt good to get out now and then. Somewhere in there I turned seventeen, an anxious and angry state: anxious to see the end of a long childhood and angry that it did not go the way I thought it should.

At seventeen, I decided I needed a car, so I too went to work at the burger place in the Restola, the place that had winked and laughed at my plan to leave, the place that had taunted me that I would be back. It was right, *so what.*

Day by day, we settled into a fragile, uneasy peace that was not quite healthy, but it gave us a good front to which to cling. Day by day, I regained a semi-comfortable routine between working, playing, sleeping and the occasional nothing date, spending as little time as possible with my parents. Lula still assumed a dominant role, spending most evenings at our house, watching TV with my mom. The way Lula threatened me would always leave a bitter taste, so my evening shift at the burger job was perfect. As long as I slept at home, that was good enough for Lula and everyone else.

Elvia went to work at the Restola as well, lasting a couple of weeks before deciding it was bullshit and going back to cooking and cleaning for her parents. I stuck it out and even grew to like it. It wasn't a dream job, but when I bought my first car, an eight-year-old hatchback with a tape deck and 114,000 miles on it, co-signed by my mother, that made any job worth it. I named my beautiful new car Belinda and never thought it strange that of all of my family, friends, teachers or acquaintances, it was a second-hand car that gave me the first real sense of adult direction I ever had.

TEN

"Anybody cute come in tonight?" said Elvia.

"Elvia, nobody cute ever comes in." I rubbed my right temple, massaging the headache that was spreading its way across my skull. It was my lunch break and we were sitting in the lobby of the Restola, on a modular plastic bench among potted palms, bulletin board displays of local and regional recreational spots, map boards, payphones and message boards flashing weather and road conditions. Across the lobby from the burgers was a minimart and a Taco Bell. Next to that was the western wear store where my mom worked. Behind us was a coffee shop, a laundromat and restrooms. Upstairs was a movie theater, a steakhouse, arcade, Subway/Baskin Robbins, an auto/truck parts store and the beauty salon where Lula worked. They cut men's hair there, too. Outside was another building with a bunkhouse and showers for the truckers and across the endless parking lot was a motel. Who would not want to stop there? We had everything.

Everything in the lobby was smooth and fresh, clean lollipop colors and smooth, kiddie-proof edges. An exhausted-looking father dragged a screaming little boy out of the minimart, through the lobby and out the double doors, letting in a blast of winter night wind that cut right through the sweater I was wearing over my uniform. Elvia's chatter was getting on my nerves tonight, and I was having trouble keeping my irritation to myself. *What time is it?* Fifteen more minutes.

"Sure they do!" Elvia trilled. "Cute guys gotta eat, too!"

"Then why did you quit?"

" 'Cause it's a shit job and I don't see how -"

"Nevermind." I knew where this was going and I was in no mood for it.

"Let's go outside so I can smoke."

"No way! It's freezing out there."

"You're wearing a sweater."

"And I'm freezing. I'm not going out there."

"Look, there's Craig Martin," said Elvia, forgetting her cigarette. "And he's going for burgers! You're missing out!"

"Yeah, I need to go out with a guy who's already got one kid and two nose rings. Or is it the other way around? Sounds like more your type than mine."

"What is your type? You hate everybody you go out with."

"When I see it, I'll let you know."

"You wanna be a virgin all your life?"

"Shut *up.*" I flushed and looked around. *What time is it?* This game of hers was getting old, her little search for someone to whom I could lose my virginity. "Oh wow, Elvia, I just remembered, you were in my dream last night."

"Yeah?"

"Yeah. It was really weird. Me and my parents were moving into a big old two-story house somewhere, it was huge. All these long, dark hallways going everywhere, like this old farmhouse that was practically falling down. Like no one had lived in it for a long time."

"Just you and your parents?"

"Yeah. Then right after we move in, you guys moved another house out next to ours and lived there. Yours was smaller but it needed lots of work, too. Then I was at a lake -"

"The reservoir?"

"No, a different lake, I don't know where, with my mom. We were watching Steve and my dad sailing on the lake, but they were in different boats, like they each had their own boat. Then there was a whole bunch of sailboats on the lake, so many we can't tell which ones are Steve's and my dad's and my mom's getting worried 'cause they were so far out. She keeps asking me if I could see them. I couldn't, but I said I could, just 'cause she was worried."

"Lookit that guy," Elvia said, pointing out a tall, blond man in a gray pinstripe suit and slicked-back hair, no tie, who stood with hands on his hips, staring at a message board reporting high winds on Highway 58. "D'ya think he's lost?"

"Hmm."

"He looks more pissed than lost," she said. "He's chasing someone."

"Dressed like that?"

"Yep. He came home from the office and found a note from his wife saying *see ya* and he's hot on her trail."

The pinstriped blond man looked to his left, toward the coffee shop, to his right at the lobby doors, back to the coffee shop. He looked at his watch, turned right and marched out the doors.

"Come on, let's see what he drives." Elvia jumped up, excited, shouldering her purse.

"Forget it! It's cold out there."

"Then I'll be back!" She skipped out after him, curly black hair swinging behind her.

No you won't. She'll follow him out, she'll stop for a smoke, then she'll run into some guy. Craig Martin was probably still here. I had to go back to work in a minute. Sipping my soda, I watched the travelers going in and out of the Restola, amazed at the varieties of people who came through there, such as we never saw in town, right across the freeway. People-watching was something I never appreciated before going to work there.

That time of year, it was mostly truckers and retirees, not so many families. That time of night, mostly truckers, or the infrequent local, for the arcade or the movies. Most of the retirees were tucked into the motel or their giant RVs by now. The whole place felt so un-Wattlesburg, sitting there in the lobby like that made me feel I belonged to something beyond Wattlesburg, something removed from it without having to leave it.

"Hey Pattie, howzit goin'?"

I looked up at Steve's best friend, Roger, who had a marijuana-and-alcohol laced grin spread across his lumpy face, wearing a black Jim Morrison t-shirt. Roger's round head didn't match his thin body. He was already getting a beer-and-fries gut, but his arms were skinny and it was still a body longing to be fatter to match the head. He made me uncomfortable because he looked lost without Steve, and he always acted like he wanted to say something to me, but didn't know what and didn't have the guts anyway.

"Okay, Roger." I answered back, standing up and pulling my big purse over my shoulder. "I gotta get back."

"Hey Pattie," he said, pausing for a second. "D' ya think I'm too old to get a job where you work?"

"Huh? You're gonna get a job here?" I didn't like this idea.

"Wull, I dunno." His words were a little slurred and his I-don't-care attitude was a little forced. He jammed his hands in his pockets and looked everywhere but at me. "I been thinkin' 'bout gettin' a job, maybe."

I shrugged and walked away, waving a halfhearted goodbye. Roger was something I didn't need, now or ever, there or anywhere. He needed something, but it couldn't be me. I needed a lot of things, none of them Roger. Some might think we would have gravitated to each other, having Steve's death in common and all that, but please, anyone but Roger. Even his feeble attempts felt like something he felt obligated to do. It would be easy enough to go to him, but for what? A substitute for nothing. Just another nothing date.

After nine o'clock, the restaurant was almost empty. I was behind the counter, waiting while a frail, white-haired couple in matching mint green polyester nattered between themselves over the menu choices. Trying hard not to tap my fingers. A haggard-looking trucker stood behind them, staring at the menu with his arms folded. I could tell he was a trucker by the grimy cap on his wet hair (fresh from the bunkhouse showers) and the way his foot tapped, still keeping time with the road, causing the keys on his belt to jingle. I recognized his brand-new plaid shirt from the western store across the lobby, it still had square creases from the wrapper. *Is my mom working tonight - did she sell him that shirt?* Shirt from Mom, dinner from me, isn't that cute. He carried his old, dirty shirt in a ball under one arm, then caught me looking at him and looked surprised. Uh-oh, it was nothing, I just zoned out for a minute there and he happened to be in my line of sight. It was just something to do while I waited for the old people.

The mint-green oldies were now nattering at me. It took a bit, but at last, everyone had everything straight and they shuffled off. The trucker stepped up and ordered two cheeseburgers, two fries, onion rings, apple pie and coffee for here, please. He looked about twenty years older than me. Thirty years, maybe, with a weariness about him that I used to know well. But I felt better now, and he looked like he hadn't felt better, ever. I repeated his order into the mike, punched the cash register and announced a total with a no-nonsense expression of arched eyebrows and pursed lips. It was one of my favorites.

"Oh," he said, fumbling for his wallet. "You prob'ly want some money, huh?"

"Yep." I held out my hand while he fumbled. "You gonna eat all that by yourself?"

He smiled and looked right at me while he fished bills out of his wallet, but he had to drop his eyes to see what he was giving me. I took his money, gave him change and wished him a nice evening without looking up. "Oh, I'm certainly gonna try," he said. He had kind of a drawl, not enough to quite be Southern, but somewhere out there. He hesitated, as if he wanted to say something else. "Um, you too. Thanks," he said, walking off to sit down. From the back, he sagged even more years.

Elvia came back, bouncing into the restaurant with a satisfied look. I almost groaned, wishing I had thought to take some aspirin on my break. How could I get her to leave without saying, *Elvia, go home.* She hung back until I was done waiting on a young mother with an exhausted, fearful look and two little brown-haired girls clinging to her hips. "Have a nice evening," I told her as she walked away. Such a useless thing to say, but required by management.

"911 Porsche," Elvia blurted, jumping up to the counter.

"Huh?"

"That guy! The guy in the suit. Remember?"

"Oh. Okay...."

"What is your problem tonight? You're just like, not even here."

"I got a headache."

"Well no shit, working in this -"

"*Shhh!*" I looked around, behind me, but the shift leader was otherwise occupied.

"Don't worry, I'm not gonna get you fired. I know how much you *love* it here." She lowered her voice, but turned up the sarcasm.

Go home, Elvia. What time is it? The trucker in the new plaid shirt came back for a coffee refill. "I gotta go," I whispered to Elvia, even though we both knew he could get his own refill.

"I was going anyway. Bye," she chirped at the trucker, waving with a flip of her hand and rushing out the same way she bounced in.

"Bye now," the trucker laughed and stepped up to the counter. "May I have a refill, please?"

"Right there," I pointed to the pot. He hesitated again, as if he wanted to ask me about Elvia. All the guys wanted to know about Elvia.

"Uh, thank you," he said, holding up his coffee cup in salute and walking away. It still felt like he wanted to say something more, or was I just paranoid from Roger? I watched him walk back to his booth, sensing a pain that stretched from his head, through his shoulders and all the way down his spine. I needed some aspirin, now. When he sat down, facing me, he caught me staring at him again and I was embarrassed. To my surprise, he looked more embarrassed. He dove into a newspaper and I absorbed myself in my headache. "Jared," I called to the shift leader, "I gotta go take some aspirin."

"After you take care of them," Jared snapped, indicating two male teenagers who had appeared out of nowhere.

May I help you.... They couldn't be more than a couple of years younger than me. It had not been a year since I quit school, but I had trouble remembering what it was like. It was the same anxiety every time someone I knew in school came in, scared that someone would mention Steve. No one ever said much, no one really knew me. I was so far removed without having *moved*, in this limbo-land between girl and woman. Girls don't go to work and women don't live with their parents.

I sent the boys on their way and my attention drifted back to the young mother and daughters I served earlier, sitting on the opposite side of the restaurant from the trucker. The littlest girl laid her head on the table, almost in her fries, while her nervous mom stared inward and nibbled a burger. The older girl was singing softly and building something with her ketchup-drenched fries. There was something in Mom's expression that reminded me of how my mom had looked in that dream last night, staring out over the lake, looking for Steve's boat.

"Hi there," someone said, startling me. It was that trucker again, showing me how well he refills his own coffee. "Sorry, did I scare you?"

"No - yeah, I'm sorry. I just got lost in space there for a sec."

"Yeah, I know what you mean. Pretty quiet in here right now and if you're like me, that'll happen real easy when it's a little quiet. Lot noisier out there." He thumb-pointed at the door into the lobby.

"Yeah..."

"Y'know, feels more like a carnival out there than a truck stop. I'm surprised there's no clowns out there, scarin' little kids with balloon animals."

"Oh, we're more than just a truck stop. Bet you got that new shirt here."

He flushed and I almost expected him to say, *aw, shucks.* "Y' know what," he said, still blushing, "I embarrassed myself real good in there."

"Oh?"

"Yeah, I forgot I was in California and lit up a cigarette while I was standin' in line at the register."

"Can't do that here."

"Yeah, I know. You prob'ly don't know this, 'cuz you're so young, but used to be you could smoke anywhere you wanted and no one said nuthin.' Still can, some places, but less and less everywhere you go."

"Well, you shouldn't smoke anyway, it's bad for you."

"Y'know, that's exactly what the lady in there said to me? Shouldn't smoke, bad for you. But sometimes I just forget and light up automatically, y'know, 'specially when I'm tired."

"Hmm."

"I couldn't tell if she was teasin' or bein' snotty."

"Mmm."

"Uh -" He cleared his throat, as if he was nervous about an important announcement he had to make, then showed me his coffee. "I just came up for another refill."

"That'll be fifty dollars, please."

He laughed at my little joke, looked a little less tense. It was our third meeting, now he thought he was entitled to ask me something personal. "Y'know, you're a real nice girl. What's your name?"

"Pattie," I answered, pointing to the name tag on my uniform.

"Oh, heh! Oh yeah? Well, what's your last name?"

He sounded gentle and unthreatening and I felt sorry for him. There was something intangible around his eyes that reminded me of Steve and for a moment, I had a crazy vision of Steve, thirty years from now, if he had lived. No harm in telling him my name. "Monk."

"Pattie Monk," he repeated after me.

"Yeah."

"My name's Duane Baty. Nice to meet you, Pattie Monk." He held out his right hand and I shook it without answering.

"Well, you're a real nice girl and I thank you for the coffee."

"It's okay. Free refills."

"Even if I want to sit here a while longer? I mean, if you need the space I'm takin' up or somethin'."

"Are you kidding? You're practically the only one in here. It's not gonna pick up anymore tonight, much, so don't worry."

"That's real nice of you, y'know. Not everyone's as nice as you."

He said it with a sincerity that made me blush, and it threw me. He didn't seem to be trying to hit on me, he didn't even look like the type that would, and I wasn't sure what he wanted or how I should respond. Always be polite to the customers. "Well, uh, you're a nice person, too."

"It's just that when you're alone all the time in a rig with no one to talk to, it's kinda nice t' be around other people for a while, even if no one talks to you."

"Oh, you don't know anyone around here?" What a lame response. I didn't know what to say to ease his loneliness without offering too much. Maybe I shouldn't be talking to him at all, he didn't seem to want to sit down, but I couldn't hurt his feelings. He already knew my name. Did I just do something stupid? *My will-I-regret-this-later list grows and grows.*

"Nah, I'm just passin' through. The proverbial just-passin'-through. I gotta drop a load in Long Beach, then, I dunno, pick up a load east, I hope."

"Why do you hope that?"

"Oh, I dunno, really. I don't want to insult you or nuthin', but I don't really care too much for California."

"Why not? I thought everyone wanted to come to California. I never heard anyone say they don't like it."

"Well, it's all brown, for one thing. I like to see some greenery around. It's all green back east and down south and stuff, you ever seen it?"

"No. What else?"

"What else what?"

"You said, 'for one thing.' What other things don't you like about it?"

"Oh nuthin', it's alright. Have you traveled much?"

"No."

"Well, you should see some other places some time. There's lots of real nice places t' see out there. There's even some prettier places than this in California, like farther up on the coast, way up, but I don't get up there too much."

"I guess." I was trying to sound indifferent without sounding rude

"Uh, how long you been workin' here?"

"Oh, few months."

"Like it?"

I shrugged. "It's okay. It's a job." *My mom works over there*, I almost said, but bit it back just in time. It could well have been her who told him he shouldn't smoke, she said that all the time, with a lit cigarette in her own hand.

"This is a real good idea, here," he said.

"What?"

"This place. Havin' all this stuff together in one place like this, right off the freeway. I mean, I seen plenty of places, all over the country, rest stops with a bunch of stuff all together, but this is the biggest one I seen."

"Oh. Yeah, I guess." Did I sound apathetic, but not rude? I was straightening up and starting to edge away.

"Uh," he stammered, "who's Bandy?"

"Huh?"

"It says, 'Bandy's Restola.' Who's Bandy?"

"Oh. I don't know. Probably just a name, I guess."

"You never wondered about it?"

"No." Should I have? Hadn't there been something else just recently that made me feel I should know more about this town? It was fleeting, and I dismissed it before it could grab hold of me.

"Well, what d'ya think? Must be the guy that owns this place, huh?"

"I guess."

"Ain't there folks in town here named Bandy?"

"Not that I know, but I don't know everybody." *I don't know anybody.*

"Well, maybe it's just a fake name. Guy that owns a place like this must be plenty rich - there any really rich guys in town?"

"No." I laughed at his ludicrous suggestion. "Why would any rich guy want to live here?"

"I dunno," he laughed back, proud of himself for making me laugh. "I bet this Bandy guy's a real fat cat with them wraparound sunglasses and big ol' obnoxious diamond rings."

"And rides around in a stretch limo." I was envious of this fictitious person with diamonds and a limo.

"Yeah, don't you hate those things? Windows all dark so's you can't see it? Those rich guys must have lots to hide."

Are you really this cornball? "I don't know. Don't you think it'd be cool to ride around in a limo? Kicking back and drinking champagne and stuff with a stereo and TV and all...."

"Nah, y'think so, really? All the rich people I ever saw were real assholes - 'scuze me, I mean real jerks. I wouldn't want people thinkin' that about me, y'know?"

"Yeah." Contrite, stung at having shown myself to be hung up on money and appearances.

He swelled again, as though he thought he taught me something. Sipping his coffee, he smiled in a forgiving way. "How long you lived here - what's this place called again?"

"Wattlesburg."

"Wattlesburg. How long you lived here?"

"All my life."

"Hmm." He seemed to expect me to ask where he was from, but I didn't.

It was now close to eleven and the influx of customers had trickled to a dead stream. Most everyone had gone home, and no one else seemed to notice me lingering with this guy. He leaned against the counter, pulling at his fingers, reaching for a cigarette but catching himself just in time. A wilted-looking couple came in and I had to take their order, so he took his coffee back to his booth. When they had been taken care of, I looked around for something with which to look busy. I didn't want this guy - Duane, was that his name? - to feel he had to come up and keep me company. Not that it was any big deal, he was just another lonely trucker. They came in all the time. He looked harmless and I felt sorry for him. As much as I hated this town, I would always remember how alone I felt away from it, and could empathize with someone like Duane. There was a certain duty to be nice to him, at least as long as he was a customer. He was not trying to hit on me, he was just lonely.

Feeling suddenly protective of him, I snuck little looks, just to be sure he was okay. He was absorbed in his newspaper. See - he had forgotten me already. It's not like I was a brilliant conversationalist. He would talk to anyone who gave him a chance. *Look at him.* Lost, exhausted. Reddish-yellow straw-like hair stuck out from under his cap in every direction, yellowish pale skin and heavy circles around his tired eyes. What did I know about a trucker's life? Elvia's father was gone a lot, he told stories about guys who didn't even have homes because they never left the road. They couldn't stand to stay in one place long enough to write a rent check. Guys with girlfriends, even wives and kids scattered all over the place. Driving, driving, nonstop forever. I couldn't imagine a life lived that way. Did people like that really exist, or were they just stories? Was he one of those guys? He looked up from his newspaper and caught me watching him again and I was embarrassed, again.

Acting as if he saw an opportunity, he drained his coffee cup and came back for another refill. As long as I was busted, I might as well be polite, so I returned his smile. But not too warm. He stayed to chat until almost closing time, mostly talking about prettiest spots he knew in other states. He was so sad and so upbeat at the same time, I didn't know what to make of him. He was kind of funny, in a hokey kind of way. He scared me a little, not in a dangerous way, but in a fragile way, as if one more strain would shatter him.

"Y'know," he said, looking at his watch, "I just remembered I'm in California and they stop selling beer here in about twenty minutes. So I'm just gonna buzz on over across the way and get myself a beer for later and I'll be right back, okay? Can I leave this here 'til I get back? I'll be right back."

"Okay."

"Be right back," he repeated as he walked out, secure that he had safeguarded his position by entrusting me with something of his. We were getting ready to close when he returned.

"Does someone pick you up and drive you home?" he said, without sounding like a proposition.

"No, I have a car."

"Do you have someone t' walk you out?"

"What do you mean?"

"To your car. It's two in the morning, not exactly the safest time t' be walkin' t' your car all by yourself."

"It's okay, it's lit. No one ever bothers me."

"Well, it still ain't safe. Someone could. Why don't you let me walk you out?"

He said it with a subliminal authority that reminded me again of Steve, not as he was, but as I wished he could have been. Steve who always got his way.

"Okay, let me get my stuff." It was just to the car. It was bright enough, I had my whistle, it would be fine.

ELEVEN

In the cold, halogen-lit night of the parking lot, I was a little less sure of the wisdom of the situation... or whatever was developing. Inside, I had the safety of the counter between us. I was tired, and now I was wary, in no kind of mood to spend the next week dissecting all this, should something go wrong. *God. Remain in control at all costs. Be careful to stay out of his reach.*

But he looked more concerned with his grocery bag of beer, not even looking at me. It was windy, frosty cold wind cutting across the asphalt, sucking every bit of moisture from my skin and crackling with static.

"Lookit this," he said, switching sides so that he was on the same side as my oversized purse. "Y'know someone could just sneak up behind you, yank that thing right off your shoulder and take off? You always work this late at night?"

"Sure. No one's ever bothered me."

"Darlin, you walkin' 'round out here all the time at night, you gotta be careful. It ain't just purse snatchers, it's perverts and you don't even want to *know* what all."

"I'm fine," I brushed off his concern. It wasn't his job. "Besides, I got a rape whistle." We both flinched at the work *rape*, and I was embarrassed to have said it. Such images were better left uninvoked. I held up my whistle in defiance of any power the word might have, there and now. It was a large, loud chrome whistle, the kind carried by coaches and P.E. teachers all over America, rattling on a key ring that had more toys and bangles hanging from it than it had keys.

"A *what?*"

"A whistle. You blow it if someone tries to attack you." It sounded so inadequate when I said it.

"And what, Superman pops out and saves you?"

"No, it scares them away, or people hear it and help you. I don't know, I never had to use it, so I don't know."

"You really think that thing's gonna scare away someone that really wants t' get you? Someone bigger than you, or with a gun could grab that thing away from you before you could even think about blowin' it."

"Well, I'm fine," I said, indignant and feeling stripped clean of my best defense.

"Go ahead, give it a blow."

"Nah, I believe you."

"No really, I just want to hear how loud that thing really is."

I blew, as hard as I could. It was loud and shrill in the clear cold night for as long as I blew, then it died, twittering away on the wind. I looked around to see if anyone was coming to my rescue. No one, the parking lot was humanly empty but for a couple coming out of the Restola, but the wind was blowing away from them and there was no chance of being heard.

"What's all this other stuff on here," he said, reaching for my keys. I let him take them, the useless whistle disappearing among all the other little toys and contraptions that made up my keyring. Rather than one central ring to hold everything, it was a bunch of rings, each holding some kind of gew-gaw and maybe one key. I didn't need very many keys, and one little ring with three keys on it wasn't enough. I liked a lot of jingle-jangle. There was a clear plastic picture holder with a photo of Elvia and me, a tiny leather cowboy boot from my mom's store, a clear red heart with liquid glitter floating inside of it, a Bart Simpson... all kinds of stuff. You could learn a lot about a person by reading their keyring.

He shook his head and handed the whole clattering mess back to me. "How in hell d' you ever find your keys on that thing?"

"I manage." Taking back my keys, I flipped deftly through everything to my car key. We reached me car. "This is it."

"This is yours?" He sounded admiring.

"This is it. Her name's Belinda."

"Belinda?"

"Yeah. You think it's weird that I named my car?"

"Hell, no," he said, lighting a cigarette. "I know plenty of guys name their rigs."

"What's yours?"

"Nuthin'."

"*Nothing*, that's its name, or *nothing*, it doesn't have a name?"

"No name. Nuthin'."

"How come?"

"No reason. Just not important to me, I guess," he shrugged, sucked on his cigarette. "Maybe you can give it a good name."

I'd have to see it first, I almost said, but caught it just in time. He leaned on the fender, cigarette dangling from his fingers. The breeze kicked up, whipped his smoke into my face.

"Sorry," he said, waving it away from me. "Smoke follows beauty. So how come you work this late, anyway?"

"I have to, I got a car payment and insurance and stuff."

"You live with your mom and dad?"

"Yeah, I can't afford to move out yet."

"What d' you wanna move out for?" he said, a little bit harsh. "You don't wanna be on your own, believe me. Much safer stayin' with your parents. Besides, it's too expensive. You'd be strugglin' t' pay bills and rent all the time, and car payments, you'd hardly have nuthin' left over for clothes and toys and stuff. And all them scumbag types out there, after you all the time -"

"Thanks a lot!"

"That's not what I mean. I mean scumbag types that just wanna use you, the kind that likes t' prey on pretty little things like you. Best you stay with your mama and daddy 'til you get married and got someone t' watch out for you. It's a big, scary world out there."

Is this guy for real? Who thinks that anymore? I wasn't a pretty little thing, so I dismissed his concerns. No one noticed me unless I wanted them to and even then, sometimes not. Smarmy bus station clerks don't count; it was his job to notice me, the way I had to notice everyone who came to my counter. Not my fault he was a scumbag... did that circle me around to Duane's argument? I already knew it was a big scary world out there. What was it about this guy that wanted to remind me of Steve? I couldn't put my finger on it. Qualities I wish he'd had? The big brother to guide me? I really didn't want to go there. "Well, um... it doesn't matter anyway, I can't afford it. They don't charge me rent, I just pay for Belinda, and my phone and my clothes, but after that, there isn't much left. No way I could afford to pay rent, too."

"How old are you?"

"Seventeen."

He looked surprised, but tried to hide it. Did he think I was older? This was new ground for me, just chatting with a man. I had to call him a *man*, he was too old to be a *guy*, and he felt even older than he looked.

Making benign small talk with a man (old) who was not trying to crawl all over me was a new thing and I didn't know why I was doing it. He must have thought I did this kind of thing all the time. I had opportunities, there was no limit to the kinds of people who came in during the late hours. Behind the barrier of my counter, the expectations were clear, simple and safe: burgers. And the opportunities for observation were endless. Some were okay, interesting but harmless, but some were scary in an indefinable way. I thought Duane would be of the interesting-but-harmless variety. Still, I never did this, walking out with them after work. Despite what he seemed to think, I wasn't that naive. I knew it was dangerous at night, I just didn't like to think about it. It wasn't that he had anything interesting to say, most of what he said was depressing. The way he shot away my whistle security blanket, I was glad he was here. I didn't know what kind of ground I was on, but I still believed I was in control. Why did I pick this one to protect me? There was nothing attractive about him, with his coarse, reddish hair, dirty cap, thin mustache, parchment skin and big teeth, yellow from coffee and smoking. Razor-thin, wearing that dorky western shirt. Not all truckers wear western shirts, but it seems the only people who do wear them are truckers. Are they all frustrated cowboys, or did they really think it looked good? He wasn't wearing a jacket, and he didn't look like he felt the cold.

Maybe it was because he kept coming back. Despite his negativity, his talk was free of innuendo, and he was so polite that I didn't want to hurt his feelings.

"Listen, uh," he said with a shy stammer, "Do you wanna get some breakfast? You must be tired and hungry from bein' on your feet all night."

"Uh... sure, I guess." Was this a good idea? But I couldn't get myself to say no, I didn't want to hurt his feelings. I didn't know why I needed to preserve his feelings at all, but there was such a fragility about him, it made me afraid to hurt him. *It will be fine. We'll eat and he'll go away, like truckers do, and I'll never see him again.* If I hurt his feelings, he would always remember me as a rude person - a rude *Californian* - and I didn't like that thought.

"Okay then," he said with a happy face. "Where to - there's that coffee shop back inside there, huh? Too bad we didn't think of that before we walked all this way out."

"No, I don't want to go there. Uh... there's a waffle place in town, it's open all night, let's go there instead."

"Whatever you say." He patted his shirt pocket to be sure he still had his cigarettes, then his keys, hanging from his belt. He took the last drag off the one he was smoking, dropped the butt on the asphalt and ground it out with his boot.

He walked around to the passenger side of my car, expecting to ride with me. Oh. Well... that was better anyway; my ride, my game. I wouldn't want to get in his rig. I unlocked the car, tossed my visor in the back seat and off we went.

There was only one road connecting the town to the Restola, Martinez Valley Road, running in a straight line through the middle of town as if it wanted to get through there as fast as possible, then up over the hills to Highway 1 and the ocean. I wished I could go there now, *alone*, sit on the beach and watch the dawn come in. *I should do that sometime.* I had only been to the ocean twice, and not since I was twelve. I wished, but in reality, I wasn't that intrepid.

The trucker sat next to me (*there's a strange trucker in my car, how did that happen?)* staring silent out at the low-slung, rundown buildings we passd, flanked by wrecking yards and struggling repair shops, flat-roofed houses with their dead lawns and chain-link fences. We were already becoming a desert monument, wind-stripped and sandblasted and resigned to the end, nothing left to do but wait while the elements finished grinding down what little was left. I was embarrassed for the town. Duane made an occasional superficial but polite comment, keeping his real impressions to himself.

Selma's Waffles was a sharp contrast to the coffee shop at the Restola, where everything is perky-new-looking. The travelers never came to Selma's, it's not visible from the freeway. The Restola coffee shop had hanging silk plants, faux stained glass and youngish waitresses in country-cute aproned calico uniforms. It even had hostesses, dressed in polyester pantsuits that made them look more like flight attendants than coffee shop hostesses.

On the other side of the freeway, Selma's Waffles was more of a time-warped mausoleum, staffed with aged career waitresses and stomped-on ex-housewives who looked more like prisoners serving time in waitress hell. A fly buzzed around the donut platter and the stacks of thick white coffee cups, cracked and stained with decades of thick coffee. Everything in the place was rotting. The waitresses moved zombie-like in the stark light while their world decomposed over their heads. When we were seated and given coffee and menus, Duane brought the conversation back to personal things.

"So, d'ya go to school?"

"Nah, I dropped out."

"How come?"

I shrugged my shoulders. "It was boring."

"Boring?"

"Yeah." I studied my menu and hoped he would drop this line of questioning.

"Well. I dropped out too. Too many years ago," he said, looking dramatically off in the distance. "And I been sorry ever since."

"How many years ago?" I demanded, eager to deflect the conversation from myself, ignoring the part about being sorry.

"Prob'ly 'fore you were born. Makes me an old man, don't it?" He smiled.

"No," I gave a nervous laugh. What as I supposed to say? Even in the harsh light, his age was indeterminate. Much older than me was the closest I could get. He was fishing for a compliment and I resented being asked to play that game. Whatever was going on was extremely tenuous and he became more uninteresting with every word he spoke, brother substitute notwithstanding.

"Yeah, it does," he said for me. "You're still a baby. You haven't even had time to be hurt by anything yet."

"How do you know?" *Be careful, don't give him a reason to probe.*

"It don't show in your face the way it shows in mine."

I shrugged again and bent over the menu, hiding my face. *He thinks I can't appreciate someone else's pain. I'm not going to tell him anything, he can go to hell. He doesn't deserve to know my pain, I'm not going to give him the gratification of giving me comfort and sympathy.* I had nothing to prove, so I would keep my dead brother to myself.

After the waitress took our orders, he picked up his story where he left off and I felt bad for not paying attention. Hands wrapped around my coffee cup, I tried to look interested in his dismal tale of a lifetime of financial woes, rig woes, child support and ex-wife woes, credit card and back tax woes.... All this plus the constant repairs on his old broken-down rig and other costs of life on the road and he was drowning in debt.

I felt sorry for him again, and it was uncomfortable. *Maybe I should pay for my own breakfast.* His desperation was palpable, as if it was a third person sitting in our booth. He told me he was put in this hole by his ex and his father's debts and kept there by his rig, because it was the only way he had to make a living. What else was someone like him supposed to do? Everyone wanted to hire the young kids, the college grads, so that left him with his rig or suicide.

I almost choked on my coffee, startled at such a horrible word dropped in such a casual way in a public place over breakfast. Was this something I should worry about? If I wasn't nice to him, would he commit suicide?

"Don't worry," he laughed in a humorless way that left me unconvinced. "I ain't the type. My mama raised me to face up to my responsibilities. I had heavy responsibilities put on my shoulders when I was younger than you and it growed me up quick. Real quick."

Then why bring it up at all? I was groping for something to say to alleviate my discomfort and get him off this macabre subject. Why was he telling me this stuff - what did he expect me to say? I was gloriously grateful when the waitress brought our food and I could busy myself with something other than trying to think of something intelligent to say. The intensity of his personal revelations embarrassed me. I hoped he wasn't expecting me to do the same. His purpose was unclear, and I felt nothing for him but pity. He was nothing like Steve - what was I thinking? First, I pitied him for being lonely; now I pitied everything about him. *He's got balls if he thinks I'm going to tell him anything.* But look at the things that almost jumped out of my mouth. Nothing about him suggested someone to whom I would want to unburden, but at the same time, here was someone who knew tragedy so well that he might be the one person who understood what I went through.

He attacked his huge breakfast as if he had not eaten in days. Didn't he just eat a big dinner at my burger job? I did the same to my own breakfast, just wanting to get this whole encounter over with as fast as possible and get the hell out of there.

He said little else for the rest of the meal, making casual comments about coffee shop food and other road fare. I answered in monosyllables, trying to pace my eating with his so we would finish at the same time. The waitress came back, took away our plates and left the check.

"D' you want a piece of pie or some more coffee or somethin'?" he said when the waitress had carried off our dishes.

"Uh, no thanks. I gotta get home before my mom starts to worry."

"Yep, always gotta think of your mama."

I felt obligated to reach for the check, but he picked it up himself before I could decide how to go about it. He acted like he intended to pay for the whole thing, so I decided not to worry about it. I trailed behind him to the cash register, still feeling I should pay for mine, but unsure how to offer. Fumbling for the right words in my head, I waited for the right opportunity but before one came, he paid for it himself and it was too late. I peeked in his wallet and saw plenty of cash, so it was probably fine, but I still felt funny for not having offered.

We drove back to the Restola without speaking. I was too tired to try anymore, wiped out from spending most of the night on my feet and tired of his company. Making conversation with someone with whom I had nothing in common was hard work. He had no trouble talking to me (talking *at* me) and that made it more difficult. The things he said to me were too frightening to pursue. I had nothing to say beyond the inane pleasantries I learned on the job, but which had run out as soon as the burgers are served.

"Why don't you stop right here," he said when we reached the parking lot entrance. "I'll just get out here. You don't wanna be drivin' through there, maybe get a flat tire on a broken bottle or somethin'."

I left the engine running but he made no move to get out. "You have no idea," he said, not turning to look at me, "how good it is to talk to someone like you."

Again, I had nothing to say to that. What did he mean, someone like me? A burger joint counter girl? I didn't like the direction this was taking, I wanted to get out of this and go home. Gripping the wheel with both hands, hoping to promote a *gotta go now* attitude, I leaned a little away from him, thankful for the stick shift and hand brake between us to act as firebreak. I wanted to pull up the brake handle, but that might make him think I wanted to stay and chat. I was glad I had the sense to stop under a street light. He made no move toward the door, or toward me, just stared straight ahead with one hand lying forgotten on his thigh and the other twisting his hair, elbow propped against the window.

"I just wanna say I think you're the sweetest girl I met in a long time... in a lotta years... and I thank you for puttin' up with me all night and listenin' to my sob stories. You didn't have to do that and I'm sorry I put all that stuff on you." He laughed, a short, chilling chuckle. "Yeah, I'm sure you really impressed the hell outta her, Duane, you sorry sonovabitch."

"No, it's okay," I said stupidly. As much as I wanted him out of my car, I felt obligated to cheer him up before he went, or at least before he started to cry. He looked close to it and I had no idea how to deal with that. The look of complete defeat on his face reminded me of how my father looked in the hospital.

He shook it off and turned to face me with a smile. "You are the sweetest thing," he said. "Oh, hey, I saw some signs off the highway when I was comin' in tonight, for fishin' and stuff, is there a lake around here?"

"There's the reservoir up outside of town."

"Out that way?" He pointed toward the hills rising to the west, hills short and rounded, bare slopes lurking dark in the blue-black night.

"Yeah."

"Bet it's nice there, huh?"

Again, I shrugged. "It's okay. Nothing up there but the reservoir, rest of it's all brown 'cause of the drought."

"Oh. I guess I was imaginin' someplace with a lotta willow trees and bass boats. Folks fish up there?"

"Yeah, and go boating and skiing and stuff."

"Sounds real nice. Maybe I'll go on up and take a look at it tomorrow. Sure be nice to look at some water for a change, 'stead of road. Would you come with me?" He said it in a somber tone designed to pluck at my pity. "Please? Sure be nice to have the pleasure of your company for a little while longer 'fore I gotta hit the road again."

"Um, sure, I guess," timid, still gripping the wheel, feet on the brake and the clutch. *Why not,* he just sounded so damned pitiful I couldn't turn him down. *Then he will go away, what will it hurt, take him up there and he goes away to put his troubles on someone else at the next truck stop.* My feet were going to sleep, if I didn't move them soon, they were going to slip off the pedals and send the car lunging forward, with my feet too dead to find the pedals again and stop it.

"Alright then, that'll be real nice. Why don't you pick me up right here. What time?"

"I don't know - what time?"

"It's up to you."

Quick calculation, it was four-thirty now, I had to be at work at six that night, so if I picked him up at two-thirty, I could still get about eight hours of sleep. It would be out in open daylight in a public place and I could end it anytime by saying, *I have to go to work now*. "How about two-thirty?"

"Sounds great. See you then, right here."

"Okay."

"I'll be waitin'. Bye now," he said, and got out. He stood in the weak light of the street lamp, bag of beer under his arm, waving and watching me drive away. His slouched, skinny body and sagging clothes made him look as if he was trying to shrink into himself, unprotected against the cold and the encroaching dawn like an ancient vampire, too close to the light.

I gave him a feeble answering wave, wondering as I stomped my left foot awake, *how in hell did I get myself into this?*

TWELVE

Introduce myself to a needle full of heroin
ooh, we've never met before... I didn't know we wanted to
Hold the needle in my right hand, focus on my left arm
where I've tied a tourniquet just below the elbow
is this right, or should it be above the elbow?
Watch a vein pop up... flick it with my fingers to help it along
hold up the hypodermic, study its contents
the heroin is red, like blood, I'm glad it doesn't look like a lot
hold the needle upright, careful get out all the air bubbles
just like in the movies
bring it down to my arm
hesitate
I don't want to do this, but I have to
this could kill me and I don't want to die
but it's gone too far not to finish
Poke the needle into the vein and empty it
it really doesn't seem like much
but I still pray I haven't just killed myself
I once heard the high was ultimate
sit back and wait for it
the rush comes but without the intensity of legend
spreads out from the vein and tickles every cell in an apathetic way
disappointment meets apprehension
maybe my fear undermines the effect
as long as I'm conscious I know I'm alive
sudden shift from death to erotica
an introduction to someone, have we met before
do I have to tell him about the heroin
tall dark and elegant
and mutually appealing
and over before anything can begin

* * *

Shit, can't even lose my virginity in my dreams. At the rate I was going, that was the only way I was ever going to lose it. I wondered if the heroin dream has something to do with that man I was supposed to see later.... *Boy, do I not want to do this.* Last night's lack of enthusiasm was now hearty regret. *What was I thinking?* I could have made up a thousand excuses for not going on this outing, without hurting his feelings. Not a date, I refused to call it a date. *What time is it?* Quarter to two.

What if I just forgot about it, didn't show up at all? Would he remember, or care? He might. And he might show up at my burger job and make a big deal about it. Everyone who worked in the Restola, including my mother and Lula, would hear about it. The whole thing had to be kept secret, or I would never hear the end of it. Just get up, show him the reservoir and send him on his way.

Martinez Valley Road headed east through town, under the freeway to the Restola. From the Restola side of the freeway, the road disappeared into deserted orchards, populated with stumpy remnants of the drought. Here and there, an old grizzled survivor squeezed out a few stunted oranges, on branches bent to breaking by their own dead weight.

It was ten minutes to three when I pulled up to last night's street lamp. There he was, looking a little anxious at my tardiness. He gave me a relieved grin and I reached over, unlocked the passenger door and let him in.

"Sorry I'm late, I overslept a little. I was so tired last night."

"I know, it's okay," he said. "I'm sorry I kept you out so late."

"Oh - it's okay." I wasn't used to being apologized to for something like that.

"I wasn't really expectin' you t' show up at all. Why should you? Pretty girl like you can spend your time with anyone you want. Why should you waste any time on me?"

Brrr, I shivered at his accuracy. He was expecting me not to show up. I could have gotten away with it.

In the harsh daylight, he looked like hell. His pale, cheesy skin was lined and blotchy, making him look even older. Frizzled straw hair stuck out in every direction, from under the same grimy cap, same shirt as last night, now wrinkled in every direction instead of just in squares. The sad part was, he seemed like a nice guy, almost the kind of guy who would do until somebody better came along, but for his age and his stomped-on looks. Even a haircut, some real clothes and a long rest wouldn't help him.

It was a ten minute drive from the Restola through town, to the turnoff that goes up to the reservoir. Like Duane, the town looked older and more worn-down under the scrutiny of high afternoon.

"Looks like things are depressed around here, too - what's this place called again?"

"Wattlesburg."

"Yeah. How'd it get a name like that? You know what a *wattle* is?"

"What?" I didn't think I wanted to know, but he would tell me even if I don't ask.

"It's that red skin stuff that hangs down from a turkey's neck."

"Gross! No, it isn't."

He laughed. "That's a wattle."

"How impressive, to live in a town named after a turkey neck. Then again, can you think of a better name for all this?"

"It's like this all over the country. The only stuff that's survivin' in little towns like this are the roadkill-eaters, y' know, wreckers, tow trucks, cemetery monuments, that kind of thing. Stuff that feeds on death and dyin'."

"Oh. I thought you were gonna say it's like this all over the country, places names after turkey necks."

He laughed again, and I marveled at the luxury of a man laughing at my jokes. The car radio was tuned to a top-forty station out of Fresno and Paula Abdul was singing.

"That the kind of music you like?" he said with distaste.

"I guess. There's only four radio stations around here and this is the best one."

"That's too bad. Who's that singin'?"

"Paula Abdul. I like her, she's okay."

He laughed. "You're kiddin'. Paula's my ex-wife's name. What's on the other stations?" He twisted the dial through the static until he found Reba McEntire. "There y' go," he said with the satisfaction of having shown me something important, leaning back in his seat with his hands folded on his belly. "That's Reba. Now ain't that a sweet voice? That's God's music there - girl country-western singers."

I curled my lip but said nothing. He listened in smiling silence, worshiping his country queen. The next song was a male singer, so he twisted the dial again to a fast-food commercial.

"That one's all news."

"Forget that." He went back to the country station. The same male singer was still on, so he turned it off.

"You don't like guy singers?"

"They're alright, I guess. I just ain't much interested in listenin' to 'em. It's too easy to get caught up in tryin' to be just like 'em. I'm just an old romantic, I guess," he said with a chuckle that was meant to be rakish, but was only sad.

Gag. Both at the thought of him being romantic, whatever that meant, and at his taste in music.

"I used t' try and live up to the guy singers," he continued. "Y' know, honky-tonkin,' drinkin' and fightin' and fallin' in love every other night with whatever girl's willin' to dance with me all night. Cryin' in my beer, just like the song, the next night when she don't want me no more, that whole thing. I guess too many years of that stuff just wore it all outta my soul. Now, I'd be happy with just a little relief now and then and a cold beer after a hard day, or if nuthin' else, a shady place for my coffin."

Had I been eating or drinking something, I would have choked on it. Not ten minutes into this and he was already talking about death. Death, his own. Isn't there some old story about a lifeline to a drowning man? Was that the role he was trying to play? Was I equipped for that?

"Now I only listen to girl singers. Loretta Lynn's my all-time favorite, my all-time favorite song is 'Love is the Foundation.' You ever hear it?"

"No."

"It's the perfect song for slow-dancin' in your dreams. Everything I know 'bout women, I learned from Loretta."

"Everything?" It was a scary thought. I didn't know this woman.

"Well, just about. I ain't sayin' I know everything about women, not even, just what little I do know, I learned from Loretta. Nevermind, I know it sounds stupid, and it's prob'ly why I don't have a lotta women chasin' after me. I'm lucky you're puttin' up with me at all."

Definitely.... The two-lane road wound up through the hills and the town faded out from under us. The winter hills were more dead than the town, a few lonesome, bent oaks here and there clinging to the dry soil, leafless and fighting the earth for water.

"D' you come up here a lot?" he said.

"Mmm." Non-committal.

"Seems like everything 'round here's just dyin' for water, even the lake right there."

"Yeah, look how low it is. I swear, it never rains here."

"Yeah.... I always think about somethin' that's like an oasis, y' know, green grass, lotta shade trees, cattails, that kinda thing, whenever I think about a lake."

I laughed. "Not around here."

"No, I guess not."

I pulled into the rec area parking lot overlooking the green-brown lake. There were a couple of boat trailers parked next to each other in the small lot, each hitched to a pickup. No one else.

"What the hell does that say," he said, pointing to the sign at the parking lot entrance. "Tesuh- Tesca-goola Reservoir?"

"Tequesquito Reservoir."

"Te -ge -"

"*Te-que-squi-to*," I corrected him, with enuncuation clear and pointed.

"*Tekeskeedo* Reservoir. What the hell kinda name is that?"

"Spanish."

"Figures. Hardly nuthin' in California ain't got a Mexican name."

Spanish. I decided not to answer his subtle slur, but I filed it away. We got out of the car and walked toward the small market and the boat launch.

"See there," he said, indicating the four-wheel-drive pickups. "Just like the big rigs."

"Huh?"

"Just like your rigs. Pickups come in all class of models, just like rigs. You should see some of the rigs out there, *expensive* like you wouldn't believe, and they got everything, they're like rollin' houses almost. Mine's definitely bottom-of-the line and it was used when my daddy bought it. Same with pickups. It all comes down to trucks and every man's gotta have one. Every man wants to be king of the road and trucks say it best."

"Oh." What was he talking about?

There was no sun, all was gray under a blanket of high clouds. It was cold and I hoped the wind would not start blowing. Inside the market, he bought a beer for himself and a diet Pepsi for me. This time, I didn't feel bad standing by while he paid, feeling cranky about being here at all. *What time is it?* Three fifteen. Two more hours to kill before I had to go to work.

"Where to?" he said, outside the store.

"I don't know, where do you want to go?"

"It's your territory, darlin'. I don't know what's here."

You're the one who wanted to see it, was my sour thought. "We can walk over there, I guess," indicating the boat launch. All guys want to look at boats. We walked around, watched one boat come out and one more go in. He identified them for me, told me about his dream of owning a nice bass boat one day. *BFD* was my mean thought. I was trying to tune him out. Already, I had learned to recognize when he was going into a long story and I was still mentally exhausted from his stories the night before. He was trying to ask me if I liked to fish.

"Huh?" I was embarrassed at being caught not listening to him again.

"Fishin'! Do you like t' fish?"

"I don't know, I never been."

"Never?" He was incredulous. "With a nice place like this right here? Doesn't your daddy or anyone fish?"

"Nope."

"Whaddaya know." He sighed, sorry for me. Another thing he would have to teach me someday, I could tell he was thinking. The delights of fishing. "Me and my old man used t' have a boat, not a real nice one, kinda old, but it worked. My ex-wife sold it while I was out on the road once - that was back when we was still married - sold it right out from under us without sayin' a word about it."

"What a drag," I obliged, to prove I was still listening.

"Yeah. It always stayed at my place, my old man never took it out when I was gone and I didn't even find out about it 'til I got home."

"Hmm."

"I was *livid* when I found out, too."

"I bet."

"She tried t' justify it by sayin' she and the kid didn't have no money for food, but I knew better. I always gave her more than enough t' last, if she was careful and besides, the kid stayed at Paula's mom's most of the time, 'cause she was always too busy sittin' around some bar t' be raisin' our kid."

"Wow."

"I know where the food money went and where the boat money went - into her liver and up her nose." He paused, looking at the lake with an expression of self-loathing. "I ain't real proud of what I'm about t' tell you, here."

Then please, don't tell me. I reached into my jacket pocket, where my keys were, turned to check on Belinda. Still there, within reach.

"I was so mad at her," he continued, "that I punched her - I ain't never hit a woman before and I never want to again, it ain't right, but believe me, I couldn't help it. I had t' knock that smirk off her smug face." He shook his head, still looking away from me. "I just hit her the once, just knocked her down, but she still had that smirk on her face, even there sittin' on the floor with her jaw swellin' up and wipin' the blood off her lip and I said to her, 'maybe if you charged all them guys you pick up when I'm out, like any other self-respectin' whore, you wouldn't run out of food money.' See, she was like that, she was always bringin' 'em in the back door when I was barely out the front. I was always true to her, even on the road. I could never understand why she couldn't do the same for me back home."

"Hmm." This was getting more and more uncomfortable. What was I supposed to say to such revelations?

"She just jumped up and came flyin' at me, screamin', with those long, fake red nails. Those fake nails cost money, too. To this day I hate red fingernails on a woman."

"Hmm," I repeated, hiding my own bitten and unpolished nails in my jacket pockets.

"I just ran outta the house and left her there and I only seen her once more after that, at her lawyer's office, when I signed the divorce papers. 'Cause I hit her, they made me give that slut alimony and child support and I had t' give up visitation rights to my little girl."

"How awful! How could she make you give up your kid?"

He sighed and ran his eyes over the hilltops surrounding the lake. "It's for the best. She lives at Paula's mother and stepfather's house and they're givin' her a better upbringin' than Paula or I ever

could. I send her a little present now and then, but I don't put who
it's from and she prob'ly don't even remember me anymore. Wanna
see her picture?"

"Sure."

"Her grandma sends a picture t' my mama every year." He took
out his wallet and showed me a picture of a smiling, gap-toothed little
girl with unruly reddish-blond hair and glasses with pink plastic
frames.

"Oh, she's cute. You never get to see her? Does she live far
from you?"

"Nah, she lives in St. Louis, too. I just think it's best for
everyone if I don't see her."

"Does your mom get to see her?"

"Yeah, she sees her at Christmas. I usually ain't home at
Christmas, so it works out."

"You don't go home at Christmas?"

"Nah... no reason to, really." He lit a cigarette and we left the
boat launch, wandering over to the jetski rentals. "Just bad memories
at Christmas and I can get them pretty much anywhere."

"Don't your parents miss you?"

"Nah, they're divorced and got their own problems. My mama
still scrubs floors, she's sixty-one years old and still out every night,
scrubbin' floors. She looks so old and worn out, it breaks your heart
and there's nuthin' I can do about it. I'm already squeezed too tight t'
help her much and seein' her just reminds me of that. I don't even go
home that much - I can't really call it home, I just sleep on my
mama's couch when I'm there. She still takes care of my daddy, too,
even though they're divorced. He's just an old broken-down drunk,
half-senile, lives in one room and just sits there all the time, drinkin'
and starin' at the boob tube. She even goes over on Christmas and
gets him cleaned up and takes him to church, fixes him Christmas
dinner, gives him a reason not t' shoot himself."

"Huh?" I caught myself wandering again, but those last words
jerked me back to attention.

"Yeah, you know how it is with old drunks. Well, prob'ly, you
don't. Always got one itchy finger on the trigger. He kinda went off
the deep end once when I was about sixteen and I had t' take a gun
away from him. He was gonna shoot both of us, thought he'd be
doin' us both a favor, put a couple of losers outta their misery, only I
didn't wanna die, so I had t' stop him."

"God!" I exclaimed, aghast. There it was again, now he was telling me that suicidal tendencies were a family trait. The more he talked, the more I wanted to get away from him. He had to be the most depressing person I'd ever talked to, worse than my father. But every time he alluded to suicide, I felt obligated to stay and listen to him, afraid that if I didn't pump him up, he really would kill himself and it would be my fault. I pictured him coming into the burger job and shooting himself right in front of me and the whole world, after accusing me in public of disappointing him, when he just needed someone to talk to. Even before him and his pitiful stories, I had begun to realize that everyone has problems with their parents, not just me. His father with a gun was not much different than my own father running after big rigs on the freeway, except my dad didn't try to take me with him. It made me shudder, the resemblance between our fathers. How easy it was to picture mine with a gun in his hand. "That's *horrible*," was all I could think to say.

"Well, don't let it bother you. Things like are s'posed to happen t' people like me."

Then what does that make me? Once again I was tempted to tell him my own story, partly to show him he wasn't the only one who had suffered, and partly because he might just understand. But I didn't want to hear anything he might have to say about my stupid trip to L.A., or any other lectures about staying with my family, and I didn't want him to be too understanding and thought that gave us some kind of bond. I didn't want to give him that kind of look into my life.

Leaving the jetski rentals, we walked along the shore of the reservoir, past the rec area until the asphalt and cement shoreline became broken concrete slabs laying scattered and upended on the shore and in the water, as if a huge moving sidewalk hit an immovable underwater barrier and crumpled on itself. These geometric man-made slabs were more indigenous to Southern California riverbanks and shorelines than any natural rock, with our strange proclivity for lining waterways with cement.

"What did all this used t' be?" he said, picking a lazy path between the pieces of slab.

"An old ballroom, long time ago. They tore it down when part of it collapsed in an earthquake."

We climbed around the concrete chunks, trying to pretend there was something interesting to be found, but tidepools don't form among man-made rocks in man-made lakes. All we found in the stagnant puddles were rotting trash and beer cans. Leaving the slabs behind, we continued our slow walk up the beach until he sat down on the hard brown dirt, moaning as he lowered himself to the ground.

"What's the matter?" I stood over him with one hand on my hip, like an exasperated mother.

"Well, nuthin', 'cept that my legs ain't used to all this walkin' around 'n stuff. I don't do a whole lotta walkin around, y' know?" he said, winking at me.

What's that supposed to mean? I sat down beside him on the bare dirt, but not too close. One lone seagull flew overhead, flapped its way over the lake, toward the hills and the sea. There had once been a lot more seagulls, before the drought. This was never a watery region to begin with and the stranglehold of the drought added its own nails to the town's coffin. The pale gray January sky held no promise of rain. The fog high clouds were thinning and a light breeze began to stir the dead yellow grasses. Duane lit another cigarette and if this was summertime, I would have been paranoid about his fire so close to all of this dead grass. He opened his beer and handed me the soda, which was warm. I sipped a little, to be polite, waiting for him to go on with his monologue. As long as I let him ramble on, I didn't have to talk about myself. Listening to him talk about his troubles was still better than talking about me.

He hardly looked at me when he talked but when he did, it made me uncomfortable, the way I got uncomfortable when another bad choice of a date started to show himself. *This is not a date!* It was nothing overt, he hadn't said anything suggestive, and he hadn't tried to touch me, but every once in a while there was something nebulous that could almost be interpreted that way. It was just subtle enough to make me wonder if it was my imagination, or if I was just looking for excuses not to like him. I hadn't mentioned the fact that I had to go to work later. It should be worked into the conversation somewhere, but I didn't want to sound too anxious to get away from him.

"Yeah," he said, "last time I was home at Christmas, I was just about your age. They let my old man outta jail on Christmas Eve -"

"How come he was in jail?" My attention pricked up, another chilling parallel to my dad.

"Drunk driving." He stubbed out his cigarette and tried to bury the butt, but the dirt was so hard packed that he couldn't scrape up more than a little bit of brown powder. He drained his beer and set the empty can next to the cigarette butt. "Crashed his car into a Bug carryin' a couple of teenagers. No one was hurt, really, just the Bug, but he already had a few DUIs - for a while there, we was bailin' him out 'bout every Saturday mornin' - they took his license away and tossed his poor old ass in jail for six whole months, let him out on Christmas Eve. I took him home and started drinkin' with him, y' know, t' cheer him up - he was bawlin' and moanin' somethin' awful and next thing I know, he's got a pistol to his head and cryin' 'bout how his life's not worth shit 'cause he's a loser and my life's not worth shit 'cause he's my father and how he'd be doin' us both a great big favor by shootin' us both. Course, that was back when I still thought my life was worth shit."

"Wow." Wondrous, wishing I could say something a bit more intelligent, or philosophical. I hated my chronic verbal ineptitude any time a conversation got a little bit deeper than what was on TV last night. Didn't I know pain - had I not been brave somewhere? Where was the wisdom I should have gained from that?

Duane shook his head and lit another cigarette. The flame from his lighter flickered in the light breeze, flaring up and whipping around the flint as if it was trying to escape. I stared into my soda can, trying to catch the weak sunlight on the surface of the liquid through the hole in the top of the can.

"When you're only sixteen years old," he continued, "and you're on your knees beggin' your old man not to shoot you and not to blow his own head off right in front of you, it grows you up quick, real fuckin' quick. Oh, I'm sorry, darlin'," he interrupted himself.

"What?" My guard went up; I had missed something.

"I gotta learn not t' talk like that in front of a lady."

"Oh! Come on, I hear that stuff all the time. I work at a truck stop, remember?"

"Yeah, but you don't talk that way yourself. I think you gotta be the first real lady I met in a long time."

"What does that mean, a real lady? What's a *fake* lady?"

"Well, lotta women claim to be ladies. Mostly the one's that're screamin' the loudest are the biggest foul-mouthed whores of all. The filthier they talk, the more they insist that they're ladies. It's like their trashy ways make 'em so ugly that's all they got t' cling to for any kinda self-respect. I bet they don't even believe it themselves when they look in the mirror."

"Well, just 'cause you haven't heard me cuss doesn't mean I don't."

"Oh, I don't believe you could say stuff like that if you tried."

"Well, here. Shit piss, fuck, cunt, cocksucker, motherfucker. How about that?"

He laughed at me. "You're so damn cute, you prob'ly got no idea how cute you really are."

I rolled my eyes and decided the time has come. "So, um, when do you have to leave?"

"Tonight, I gotta be in Long Beach by midnight and pick up a load for Kentucky."

Perfect. I was afraid he did a local run and I might have trouble getting rid of him. I didn't want to let myself think about that. But no, he's going away for good and I could relax now, be a little kinder without danger of him getting attached. "Too bad," I said, trying to sound as genuine as possible.

"I know, just as I was startin' t' enjoy life for a change. But I got time t' take you out for a nice dinner or somethin' 'fore I go."

"Oh, I can't, I'm sorry. I gotta go to work."

"Aw, you're kiddin'. Can't you call in sick or somethin'?"

"No, I need the money."

He shook his head again and stubbed out his cigarette, leaving the butt next to the carcass of the last cigarette. "Can't argue with that. Too bad you can't just come with me"

"Yeah." Whoops, did that sound wistful? Wishful?

Wishful enough for him. "There's room for you. It ain't the fanciest rig you ever saw, but it's okay."

"What? I can't do that!" This summoned up a host of unpleasant images. Traveling thousands of miles with him, confined to a tiny cab with *him.* Those cabs are a lot smaller than they look from the ground, I knew that much from climbing around Elvia's dad's rig when we were little. He told us how those cabs can shrink by the mile, pushing into the corners of your body until you think you will never stand up straight again. My God, we would almost have to get *married* to do such a thing - that couldn't be what he meant by his suggestion. The idea was crazy.

"Why not?"

"I can't! I have a job! What about my parents? I can't just leave. I'm only seventeen - I don't even *know* you!"

He nodded, drawing circles in the dirt with his fingertip. "I know. It's a stupid idea, I know. It'd sure be nice t' have you along, though. Three-thousand mile run's a great way t' get t' know someone. You ever been to Kentucky?"

"No."

"It's pretty, you'd love it. Real green everywhere, lotsa water and trees and the hills are green and it's all woods, everything's beautiful green there, not like here."

Not like here. Someday, I wanted to go someplace that was not like here. Not like L.A., either. The restless breeze blew my hair across my eyes, trying to remind me of something, but I couldn't think what. Not the heroin needle I had held so trepidatiously over my vein in last night's dream. Why did that thought suddenly flash in my head? *Brrr.* I studied the brown, dusty hills, trying to imagine them green and covered with trees. That would be pretty; I could almost see it. But what would want to grow in such an ugly place as this, where the sun beats down unchecked and the rain doesn't? This turbid reservoir, shrinking in the unrelenting drought, had no color at all but for the bathtub rings it left around the shore as the water level receded.

Going away with him would mean he expected me to sleep with him and the idea was repulsive. Now that he had put *that* out there, it bothered me. So far, any hint of that had been absent. What would make him think he wanted me along on a trip like that? He knew nothing about me. He had hardly asked me a thing about myself. Despite deflecting every effort he did make, I now resented him for not trying harder. I knew too much about him to ever want to see him again. No doubt he would forget me by the next truck stop, where he could latch onto a new "lady," just as gullible as me.

At least things had been set straight between us. I was *so* relieved at the way he set himself up for neat, pat rejection without any help from me. He, of all people, should understand obligations. I felt the whole episode winding down, it was time for his uncomfortable revelations to come to an end and I could stop trying to think of something smart to say in return. *What time is it?* Four-fifteen.

"We should probably go, I gotta go home and change before I go to work."

"Yeah," he answered, his tone now crisp with detachment, absent expression still pointed out across the lake, as if he had spotted someone he didn't like on the other side.

Trying to hurry him along, I stood up and brushed myself off, then stared down at him with hands on my hips until he got the hint. Groaning, he heaved himself to his feet, acting as if he weighed four hundred pounds instead of about one-forty. When he had stretched and straightened himself out, he lit one more cigarette and started back to the car.

"Don't forget your beer can."

He stopped and turned around, surprised. "The park folks'll get it," he said, as if I had asked him to pick up a dead pigeon.

"Yeah, and if they see us leave it here, it's a $500 fine."

"$500!" Smoke trickled out of his nostrils, and he made no effort to pick up the can. "You gotta be kiddin' me. Fuckin' California. That's just ridiculous, you don't really believe that, do you?"

"Yes!"

"Aw," he dismissed me and started to turn away. I picked up the can myself and started back at a brisk pace. He caught up with me, took his can out of my hand and carried it to the trash himself. "Well, that wasn't so hard," he said, making fun of himself and smiling at me.

THIRTEEN

Driving down from the hills, Duane kept himself and his comments distant, already weaning himself from me, reconstructing the walls he took down for me. In the face of his retreat, my comments were more light-spirited than I had been able to muster before. Showing him what he would be missing? He turned on the country station and sulked all the way back to the Restola, not even bothering to turn it off when a male singer came on. I stopped the car at the same place I picked him up, again leaving both hands on the wheel and the engine running.

"Why don't you turn this thing off for a second," he said, reaching for the keys.

Now what? I pulled the brake handle as high as it would go. Like my rape whistle, it was a feeble barrier. I felt my precious *control* slipping away, then remembered we were parked on a main street in the middle of the day and I was still in the driver's seat. I took the keys out of the ignition and held them, casual, but out of his immediate reach.

"I wanna thank you," he said with a grave face, trying to face me in the cramped seat, "for the pleasure of your company last night and today. I been feeling real down lately, 'til you came along and cheered me up and I just wanna say that I think you're 'bout the nicest, sweetest person I've ever met and I mean that."

My face flushed, and I was still on my guard, but wondered if I should feel guilty for being so.

"You did a real good job of puttin' up with me and I'm real sorry if I gave you the wrong idea back there, when I asked you t' come along with me. You'd be perfectly safe with me, I mean, I want you as a man and all, but more I just want your company, just wanted to have your sweet face with me t' brighten up that long haul. I was just bein' selfish, that's all, I know it's a stupid idea."

He was making me uncomfortable again, saying things for which I had no smart response. Did he think I would change my mind? There were tears in his eyes and that was too much, I had to be rid of him, *now*. "Well, uh," I started to stammer, but he cut me off.

"Well, we both gotta go, so just gimme a little kiss goodbye, please, darlin'?"

I hesitated, then let him kiss me, just a little peck with my lips tight closed, and it was the most unappetizing kiss I have ever had. I could taste cigarette ash on his thin, dry lips and after a quick second, I pulled back, managed to smile a little and said goodbye, resisting the urge to wipe my mouth on my sleeve.

"Bye, Pattie," he winked and got out, stood and watched me drive off. I didn't look back as I started the car and whipped a fast U-turn out, trying not to peel out. Then I wiped his kiss off my mouth.

Even though my uniform was in the trunk, I drove home to change my clothes. I was disappointed to find my mother's car in the driveway. She didn't get off until six. Her dusty brown Vega was parked in the exact middle of the driveway, as if she was the only one here who owned a car. Inside, I could hear her in the kitchen, talking to someone. *Lula.* I was so tired. After so much time with the depressing Duane, I was almost glad to see Lula. Almost.

"Pattie?" My mother called from the kitchen. "Is that you?"

Without putting my purse down, I went into the kitchen, where they both sat at the table, drinking coffee and eating a sticky coffee wheel that looked like a day-old from the discount bakery.

"How come you're home?" I greeted my mother without ceremony.

"I had the worst headache." She demonstrated by holding one hand to her temple and closing her eyes in pain.

You are the worst headache.

"I just had to get outta there," she said. "Where've you been? Your phone's been ringing in your room."

Knowing my mother's question didn't require an answer, I ignored it and took a soda from the fridge. On my way out of the kitchen, she called after me, "Aren't you gonna say *hi* to your Aunt Lula?"

"Hi, Aunt Lula," I yelled back and slammed the door to my room.

* * *

That night, I went through my shift tight-lipped and anxious, not impolite but not as friendly as normal, especially with the male customers. I avoided eye contact, brushed them off and rushed them out, trying not to look up from the register for fear Duane would be there, sitting in a corner booth or standing in line, staring at me with those sad, bloodshot eyes. I kept one eye on my watch and the other on the wall clock, in case one spontaneously began to move faster than the other. Tried to use mental telepathy to move the hands; it didn't work.

I tried not to think about him, I didn't want to think about him, but I thought about him. Sad, is what I thought. He dumped so much on me that it was impossible to put him out of my mind. Now that he was gone, or going, I felt as if I had escaped something vaguely menacing. Not him, but the threat that his problems could overwhelm me as well. He was too old, he was never going to be my type and there was no need to go on with this. I would rather not admit to myself that I was so shallow as to be hung up on looks, because there were plenty of other things not to like about him, but I could never be attracted to him. The ideal ending would be him disappearing forever.

In order to get out of going out among the crowd to bus tables, I bribed one of the guys on my shift, Frankie with the stringy blond ponytail and vulgar personality, by promising him a fifth of vodka I had stashed. As it turned out, I could have saved myself the fifth, because Duane did not come back.

Frankie demanded payment that night as part of the deal. We took my car back to my house to get the bottle, because Frankie's car was an old station wagon with grimy curtains on the back windows and a muffler with a bullet hole in it that would wake the whole neighborhood. Frankie said he liked his car loud that way because it sounded mean and he liked the story that came with it, even if it wasn't his story. Frankie was so full of everyone else's stories that the rest of us thought he shot up the muffler himself and the rest was all bullshit. I turned onto my street, turned off the headlights and parked in front of the house two doors before mine.

"Stay here," I told Frankie, pulled the brake and left the engine running. I always left my bedroom window unlocked when I was out, disregarding any danger of someone else using it to get in. I tiptoed across the lawns, raised the sash and slipped inside, fetched the bottle from the back of my closet and climbed out. Closed the window after myself and ran back to the car, made a fast U-turn out of there.

"You must do this a lot," Frankie sneered. "You look like an *expert*. So what else are you an expert at?"

He tried to slip his hand between my thighs but I slapped it away, nearly driving into a curb. He laughed at me and pulled the bottle, three-quarters full, out of the bag. "You rip this off your old man?"

"Nah, Elvia's sister bought it for me. She's cool that way."

"All *right*. So where's Elvia these days?"

"Around."

"I know," he tapped my arm with the bottle, "let's go get her and we can all share this."

"Okay," I agreed and jerked away from him again. Frankie was too gross to like and Elvia felt the same way, so it was safe to let him tag along. There was no danger of Frankie and Elvia hooking up and leaving me out. This way, we got to cheat him out of two-thirds of his three-quarter bottle and laugh at him getting drunk and obnoxious over Elvia.

We repeated the same covert window ritual at Elvia's house. Frankie sat in the car and watched us, congratulating himself and no doubt making note of the location of Elvia's bedroom window. Elvia disappeard from the window, then climbed out a minute later. Her hair floated around her slim face and shoulders like black lace, curled bangs standing straight up from her forehead. She was wearing full makeup as if she had been waiting for someone to come by. She opened the passenger door and ordered Frankie to get in the back seat, and he obeyed, happy to be bossed around by her.

"What else can I do for you, babe?" he leered at her as he climbed out, then back in. "You joinin' me back here?"

Elvia rolled her eyes and threw the seat back, almost whacking him in the face. I drove us up to the reservoir while Elvia and I chatted and laughed about nothing, ignoring Frankie in the back seat. He looked a little awkward back there by himself, trying to appear disinterested while trying to figure out a way to get himself back in the center of attention. Seeing the bottle nestled on the console, next to Elvia's hip, he leaned forward, trying to sound seductive. "Hey Elvia, how 'bout we get that started?"

"Wait 'til we get there," I snapped over my shoulder.

"Come on," he reached for the bottle, but I slapped his hand away.

"I said wait!" In the same motion, I grabbed the bottle and tucked it under my seat, this time without swerving. Elvia shriekd with laughter and Frankie sat contrite, like a little bad boy. *That was good, I did that well.* I was *assertive.* Maybe with a little more practice, I could be good at it. I could have a lot more fun if I was that way. After the last twenty-four hours I needed something stupid and easy, and Frankie was an excellent choice.

In the rearview, I could see him fuming back there. This wasn't the way he planned it, I could tell. What a rare experience to watch that happening to someone else. He was plotting back there, trying to figure out how to take *control* but it was two against one, and one of us was Elvia. That's twice now that I'd slapped his hand away and he looked as if he'd like to give it right back to me. Soon enough, Elvia would be laughing at something else and he would have to get her attention again.

The car hit a pothole, bouncing the bottle out from under the seat. With my left foot, I kicked it back under place, hoping Frankie didn't try to retrieve it from the back. But he was still sitting in the middle of the seat, blocking my rear view. He really was gross. It was too bad Danny Murphy wasn't working that night, I could have asked him instead. He wasn't attractive either, but at least he was nice. Not gross, like Frankie.

"Where were you today?" Elvia was asking me.

"Nowhere. Can Maggie get us another bottle, 'cause I had to give this one to Frankie."

"How come?" Indignant shrill from Elvia.

I stopped at a red light and rubbed my temples. "Because I didn't feel like bussing tonight, so I bribed him to do it for me. Besides, I'm making him share it with us."

Dig it, they're talking about me, I could see Frankie's ego swelling in the rearview mirror. He couldn't hear what we were saying, the music was up too loud to hear anything else back there.

"I don't know why you wanna work there," Elvia said, trying to reopen one of her favorite debates, digging through her cavernous purse for a lipstick. The impossible shade of red she applied in the visor mirror made her look even more like a wild-eyed, spoiled little girl.

I rolled my eyes. This subject was one more thing for which I was not in the mood. "Because, because, because, Elvia, I gotta work somewhere so I can pay for this car and my phone and if I get promoted, I can make more money."

"Ooh, then you can be the *head* bungirl!" She snorted. "Not much more money. Why don't you just get a different job where you don't have to wear that dweeb uniform and work with such freaks?" She looked back at Frankie and we both erupted in giggles.

Now he looked uncomfortable; he knew we were laughing at him. Even in the dark, I knew his face was red. He looked like he wished we weren't girls, so he could kick the shit out of us, one at a time, but he needed to keep his cool in front of Elvia. After all, there was a bottle waiting for him.

"Every other place at the Restola pays the same and they all have stupid uniforms."

"No they don't - your mom doesn't wear a uniform."

"Oh, like I wanna work with my mom!" I turned down a dirt road winding through the darkness, over a bluff and ending at a long, low gate. We parked and got out, I took a blanket out of the trunk and the bottle from under the seat. The three of us walked down to the lakeshore in the cold, clear night, with a chilly breeze whistling around us, soft but insistent, not harsh enough to drive us away, but strong enough to show it would not go unnoticed.

Frankie lagged behind, still ignored but encouraged by the sight of the blanket. He thought it would be the four of us - himself, us and the bottle - rolling around on it together. I unfolded the blanket just enough for me and Elvia; Frankie got to sit in the dirt.

"Come on," he whined, "don't I get to sit down, too?"

"You can sit there," said Elvia, pointing to the bare ground.

He sat facing us, eager as a puppy for his bottle prize, but trying to be cool about it. How strange - I had just been there that afternoon, looking over the same lake, but everything about the afternoon was slipping farther back in time. *Was it just this afternoon?* Now that it was done, the whole episode was taking on the quality of a half-remembered dream, almost made me wonder if any of it really happened. Was there any reason now why I couldn't pretend it didn't?

Here, in a different spot than this afternoon, there were no cement edges. Here, the man-made lake was laid bare against the earth, which was in a constant fight to re-emerge from a forced drowning. The night-dark hid the drought rings and out here, away from the roads and the rec areas, the reservoir almost felt as if it was meant to be here after all. The night breeze swept up from the black water and through my hair, blowing it across my face as I drank from the bottle. The vodka burned down my throat, then became a deep warmth radiating from my solar plexus through my chest, the rays of a vodka sun insulating me against the chill.

The hills around the lake were silhouetted black against the late night sky. Round patches of luminescent clouds stretched over the hilltops on the other side of the water, pulling thinly apart in the middle for the stars to bleed through, shaped kind of like an evaporating mushroom cloud. I saw those movies, too. The bottle made its way around, Elvia and I continued our exclusive conversation, discussing nothing that gave Frankie a way in. Frustrated, he took longer and longer pulls on the bottle, listening while Elvia filled me in on what I missed on TV today. Our voices took on an echoing resonance as we grew more drunk. Elvia and I howled self-righteously at the exploits of the TV people. Frankie edged closer to Elvia, taking extra long pulls on the bottle to rebuild his balance, until she caught on and made him back off again. He moved far enough away to feel exiled but still close enough to pass the bottle. He had to lean forward to reach it, just enough to lift his butt off the ground, leaving his backside exposed to the night. The vodka was giving him a look of filmy, slit-eyed wonderment, watching Elvia's mouth move and laugh, her lips forming words he was beyond understanding. Her words were intercepted by the breeze, blending with the singing, singing, singing of the blowing grasstops and the night birds and the restless wind. The threadbare mist moved down from the hilltops, sneaking across the water, genesis of the early-morning fog.

We three grew foggier, I grew more bold, and Elvia grew more shrill. Her rapid-fire commentary continued to exclude him, my vicious laughter continued to ridicule him. Smart comments of my own followed Elvia's, each tearing a new piece from him and intended to make him feel as degraded as every asshole of a date ever had made me feel. This was truly a transformational experience for me, this was a most *transformitory* vodka. *I must write a book about this someday.*

When the vodka was gone and we had made Frankie feel sick in his soul, he crawled off in the darkness to throw up. Elvia and I ran cackling back to the car and took off in a spurt of dust, leaving him all alone on his hands and knees with his face hanging in the dirt.

walk down the street of a dark unknown city in the middle of the night
with my brother
I'm afraid I'm confused I don't know why we're here
the night city the dark doorways and the living shadows
I should feel safe with my brother but he's unpredictable and unconcerned with me
until I remember he is supposed to be dead
and his living walking presence confuses me
How can he be here, but he is, solid and real
His death must have been a dream
It was a dream!
what a magnificent feeling of relief
such wretched upheaval, just another ride on the night mare
all is right after all

the city street is deserted
shadowy storefronts devoid of commerce or life
yet I feel myself watched
not by people unseen but by the buildings themselves
each empty window a probing judging eye following my every move
I move closer to my brother but he moves away from me
walks ahead with hands in pockets
Wait here, he says, ducks into a liquor store and leaves me alone
the light from the store streams across the sidewalk
a single tiny oasis of light on the dark street
should I stand in the light where I can be seen
by whatever lurks
or should I hide in the shadows where I can see nothing
both ways leave me vulnerable
and angry at him for leaving me
in this unsavory situation
but in truth, it's so like him, I shouldn't be surprised

he comes out with a bottle in a bag and we walk on
the store owner runs out screaming Shuffle! Shuffle! over and over

out of the darkness comes a gang of sailors
run my brother down
lost in a blur of flying fists and feet
Horrified and powerless I watch my brother beaten to death
senseless and inexplicable
I want to scream but the sound strangles in my throat
they finish their murderous work and are gone
and there is my brother's dead body
lying next to the crushed paper bag
blood and liquor flow together
over the curb and down the gutter
oh God oh God this time it's not a dream
this time he really is dead

I awoke with a start, disoriented. Slowly, I recovered my awareness of being in my own bed, in my own room, and awakening from a dream. *It was a dream? Really?* At the time, I was so sure it wasn't. I felt helpless, just like in the dream. It was *so real*. How lose-lose can you get? *He's dead, he's not dead! he's dead! yup, he's really dead.* Sometimes, I hated my fucking life.

My head pounded with a hangover and I turned over to try to go back to sleep. I stayed in bed, dozing in and out, until it was time to go to work. When I got there, self-medicated with antacids and Tylenol 3 from my mother's medicine cabinet, I found that our friend Frankie told everyone that he had had athletic sex with both me and Elvia at the lake last night. I called him a liar and an asshole, but he laughed and chucked me under the chin.

"Hey baby, you look like warmed-over death. Rough time last night?" He leered, to the *woos* of our coworkers.

I flinched at his touch, burning red with anger and embarrassment. "Fuck you, asshole," was the best I could do, shoving my way past him to the counter. Why was it that he was the one left stranded and ralphing on his knees in the dirt and I was the one getting laughed at? No wonder Elvia quit this place.

FOURTEEN

But secretly, I loved my job. So secret that I only half-admitted it to myself. It wasn't the kind of job I should have liked, but it was mine and I did. It was so much better than school: I got paid, there were no grades (I either did my job or I didn't), the community and the social structure were so much smaller and infinitely simpler. At school, I was a child; at work, I was an adult. In a way, I had almost achieved what I set out to do by going to L.A. I have a *job* plus I have a *car* equaled *I am an adult*.

Work gave me a routine and an escape. Adhering to a basic routine kept my life simple. Complex or confusing issues could be solved or abandoned by saying, *I have to go to work now*.

Even an annoyance like Frankie solved itself eventually. A few days later, Frankie was fired for showing up drunk and I didn't have to listen to his taunts anymore. Once he was gone, everyone else forgot about it. No one had believed much of what Frankie said about anything anyway, they'd just enjoyed watching him harass me. Frankie had been unpopular with everyone. Along with rude and obnoxious, he mixed his lies with ugly little truths, the kind you thought no one saw, that made you squirm and laugh about yourself when you just wanted to slap his evil mouth shut. I hated him, but I also had to hate myself for getting involved with him and bringing it on myself. Same old song.

That dream about my brother disturbed me. It was the first time I had a dream where I actually stopped, took stock, and consciously decided it was not a dream. And then, it was. What a horrible mind-trick to have played on you. It was *real* - he was back, then he was dead, *again*. And then I woke up, and he was still dead. The dream was real and my life was the dream.

But what mattered was *now*, coming out of the movies at the Restola, with Elvia. Riding the escalator down to the lobby, I was not happy to see Steve's best friend, Roger, standing at the bottom of the escalator. Damn, not Roger. Same black Doors T-shirt, unkempt brown curly hair standing out like a halo around his moon-face. His eyes were at half-mast and bloodshot, and he was holding a double scoop ice cream cone. *Munchies.* He hadn't seen me yet, but unless he walked away in a hurry, he would when the escalator deposited me at his feet.

"Look, it's Roger," Elvia said unnecessarily. "He wants to go out with you so bad," she laughed, "but he's got this weird thing about your brother."

"What?" I was shocked at the accuracy of her observation. I groaned, looking back at the top of the escalator to see if I could escape, but it was too late, I was there and Roger was damn glad to see me.

"Whoa, it's Pattie," he greeted me with stoned surprise. He recovered himself and held out his ice cream cone. "Wanna lick?"

"Uh, no thanks." *Ick.*

"That's good 'cuz you prob'ly shouldn't be lickin my ice cream anyway," he drawled in his slurry sucking-and-gushing singsong. His free hand was jammed into his jeans pocket, his ice cream cone swayed carelessly, and he looked at everything around him but me.

"*Huh?* Whatever, Roger." We kept walking, leaving Roger behind. Elvia was laughing as we went out the door.

"You're full of shit, Elvia."

"I'm telling you, that boy's in love! He just doesn't know it yet."

"Oh God, I just remembered what I dreamed last night."

"Just like that?"

"Well, the sky looked just like it does now - all stormy-looking with the sun peeking out a little bit right there... that's what made me remember."

"You mean you dreamed that it's gonna rain?"

"No, I was just standing around somewhere, looking at the sky - it was kind of dark and cloudy - the clouds were really black, just like that, but kind of scattered over that way, where the sun was peeking out before it set. Then I was up at the reservoir and there was all these knives sticking out of the ground. Some guy was there, but I don't know who he was."

"Was he cute?"

"I don't know. I couldn't really see him."

"Then how do you know he was there?"

"I don't know, I just did."

"Weird, you and your weird dreams."

"What'd you dream last night?"

"I don't know," said Elvia, uncaring. "Something about a pistachio wagon."

"A *what?*"

"A big red wagon full of pistachios."

"Well, *that's* weird."

She laughed, tossing her hair. The wind picked it up and lifted it over her shoulders and in front of her face, but she grabbed it, jerked her head to fling it back into place. The black clouds broke apart and moved across the sky with the wind, rejoining and breaking again. The dual wind was laced with the cold of winter and the warmth of the promise of rain.

I looked up at the changing sky and an odd sensation ran up my back. Now I couldn't remember if I really had seen this sky in my dream, or if I'd seen it somewhere else. Then why would seeing it now trigger the memory of the dream? It was too familiar. Or was I having the dream *now*.... I looked around the parking lot, taking and evaluating as much detail as possible, looking for some clue one way or another. The asphalt expanse of parking lot stretched out under the insistent wind, holding nothing I could separate as unreal, surreal, dreamlike.... Scattered people moved back and forth between their normal-looking cars and the normal-looking Restola, huddled in their coats against the wind. Only then, staring at the Restola and trying to decide if I was dreaming or not, did I realize how often I had dreams about the Restola and all it contained. Too much of my life was being lived here. Or not enough of my life?

"Come on - what're you *doing?*" Elvia demanded, her wailing voice already dancing away on the wind. My paced had slowed to nothing, while Elvia stood next to my car, hopping up and down in the cold. "Let's *go*, it's freezing!"

Later in the evening, and the expected promise of rain still failed to manifest. It was trying, a little spit here and there that only evaporated in the brittle, dry cold. The wind whipped up and down, quiet here, sneaking up on you *there*, still insisting there would be rain, just be patient.

Later in the evening, and it was party time. I stood alone on the back porch of Elvia's sister Maggie's house, waiting for it to rain.

Inside, the stereo boomed something I didn't recognize, something from the seventies, I thought. I'd never been to a party like this before and I was on my second beer, drowning my fear of the strange and dangerous-looking people inside. Maggie's husband was a biker, and a lot of their friends were bikers, whether real or wannabe, I couldn't tell, but it didn't matter. So many knives and tattoos in one place made me feel conspicuously young and naive and I was standing outside in the cold night trying to get a grip, trying to grow up enough right then and now, to not be so scared to be at this adult party. Trying yet again to drag myself forward into womanhood. Elvia wasn't scared to be here, why should I be? I was glad I wasn't here on a date. Some people were doing lines in there, right out in the open, and I was terrified that everyone would be arrested at any moment.

Brrr, it was cold out there. I sipped my beer, trying not to go too fast, but trying to keep as warm as possible. Elvia was inside somewhere, last seen flirting with a tall, dark and buff biker wearing a black leather vest and no shirt. Shaking with the cold, I gripped my beer can with my fingertips. It popped out of my grasp and landed with a dull splat on the ground below.

Shit. I cursed myself and jumped down to pick it up. The wind charged me in a short burst, followed with a few raindrops. *Pretty measly*, I said to the sky as I walked my dirt-encrusted beer to the trash can. If I had a leather jacket, I might have felt a little more in place. Elvia had one. I would start saving immediately, but it was too late for tonight. My prissy little white nylon ski jacket with green-stripe trim looked straight out of the sixth grade.

The wind died and surged from no consistent direction, carrying raucous laughter from inside the house, then the stink from Maggie's garbage cans. I caught a brief snatch of Elvia's laugh, lilting and cackling from inside the kitchen. For a brief, astonishing glimpse, I felt a detachment from myself and my surroundings that was so complete that I was disembodied. The unfamiliar house, scrubby back yard and row of garbage cans were random shapes, unidentifiable as anything I had ever seen before. From the immediacy of standing behind Maggie's house in the cold night to the totality of the construction of my life and its place in the universe, and the multitude of layers in between, my disconnection was perfect. And then *boof*, it was gone, just like that and I was blinking and shaking my head to regain my mental equilibrium. *What was that?* I followed Elvia's voice back to the kitchen to get a fresh beer.

"There you are!" Elvia squealed drunkenly. She was wearing the tall, dark biker's arm around her shoulders like a feather boa. The beer-light behind her eyes gave her features a hardness that made her look almost old enough for her new boyfriend. Three other guys were propped against the kitchen counters, laughing and supervising while another one rooted through the cupboards.

"Aha!" the searcher roared in triumph, brandishing a tiny can of chili powder. His discovery was applauded, a shot glass was produced, and a bottle of tequila. The shot glass was filled, then garnished with a generous sprinkle of chili powder. "Who's first?"

"After you."

"No *sir*, after *you*."

"How 'bout ladies first, uh?"

They bowed in exaggerated unison at Elvia and me. My eyes must have been wide as saucers. My stomach retched at the thought and I shook my head no. "Go for it, O'Rourke," Elvia goaded her new boyfriend, shoving him in the ribs. "You first."

O'Rourke stepped forward to the jeering chorus of his colleagues. "He doesn't look like an O'Rourke," I whispered to Elvia. She shrugged and gave me an innocent smile.

With a high degree of ceremony, O'Rourke approached the shot glass, addressed it, extoled its virtues and finally, downed it. His friends applauded and laughed as he fumbled for a beer to chase it, then he was out the back door and stumbling down the steps, collapsing and vomiting in the dirt. *"Orourke,"* came the guttural sound from the poor guy, down on all fours. *"Orourke, orourke...."*

I get it. Now I was laughing along with everyone else. "Charming guy," I said to Elvia, who was already leading me out of the kitchen while the remaining friends of O'Rourke refilled the shot glass and argued deferentially over the next turn.

Outside the swinging kitchen door, I collided with a menacing-looking woman with long, straight hair and so much black eyeliner that her eyes looked like pin dots. In slow motion, the woman brought a joint to her lips, her eyes boring so deep into mine that I froze, caught and held by the authority of her glare. The hand that held the joint was wrapped halfway to the elbow in silver bracelets that shifted in layers as she moved the joint upward, hovered, then back down. The sickly-sweet marijuana smoke curled in serpentine tendrils around the woman's face, threatening to ensnare me in a vaporous awe.

Unsmiling, she held the joint out to me. I gulped, whispered, "No thanks," trying to smile as I hurried away.

I was getting that panicky feeling again, expecting the cops to come bursting through the door. *Let's go, Elvia, let's go...* but Elvia was having too much fun drinking free beer and doing O'Rourke imitations for Roger. *Roger?* Where'd he come from? It was time to get out of there. People were lying on the living room floor, spaced out and draped over one another. Elvia laughed at her own wit and Roger snickered his stupid Bevis-and-Butthead laugh. I clutched my beer, trying to be invisible. Roger held his beer the same way he held his ice cream cone, at a careless angle that could mean suds all over whoever was near him. I wanted to sneak out of the room before he saw me, but there were only two ways out from where I stood - back to the kitchen, past the spooky woman with the joint, or down the hall toward the bedrooms, and there was no telling what I would find back there.

One overweight, toothless guy with a froth of red hair and beard, lying on his back on the floor, had hold of Maggie's black cat by one hind leg. He laughed at the poor cat, who hissed and bit at his hand, trying to get away. Suddenly, Maggie came flying into the room, screaming, "Hey asshole, let goah my cat!"

When he ignored her, she stomped on his forearm, breaking it with a wicked crunch. Maggie jumped back as the cat shot out of the room and the redheaded man roared to his feet, whipping out a switchblade. I shrieked and shrank behind the doorway in horror, knowing that everyone there, especially me, was going to end up in jail.

Maggie avoided being knifed by ramming a pointy-toed cowgirl boot into his balls, just as he lunged at her with the knife. Elvia grabbed my hand and we ran for the back door, escaping as the whole place exploded into a fight that had to be broken up by the cops. Everyone left in the house when the cops get there had to be bailed out of jail, including Maggie. One more close escape that left me shaken and wanting to hide in my dark, locked room, just like my crazy mother.

FIFTEEN

picture a black-hooded snake traveling snakelike along a river of blood
My detachment is such that this is a movie, not a dream
I myself am nowhere
only the snake and the river are here
the snake moves downriver as on a surface of red glass
graceful swaying side to side
hooded head poised upright, hood-ornament style
The camera pans away from snake and blood
to vast expanse of flatland, parched and bare
Hordes of fieldworkers swarm chaotic over hardpacked brown earth
each one faceless and generic
carving Xs into the earth with a large machete

dust carved by swarming workers billows into the sky
forms an image of a woman
a mermaid
hovering overhead with long dirt-colored hair
floating smoke-like in the air
the camera pulls back and here I am, sitting in a movie theater
watching the dust-cloud mermaid movie playing on the screen
then the movie is over and it's Roger on the stage
singing, still clutching that ice cream cone
No, it isn't Roger singing, Roger is just standing there dumb
his mouth hanging open and his eyes at half-mast
ice cream melting and dribbling down his hand
It's Jim Morrison's face on his shirt that is singing
if it can be called singing
The grinning t-shirt face grumbles and growls
chews on the microphone
crunch-crunch-crunch

Instead of clapping, I raise a bell and ring
ring-ring, ring-ring

I woke to the powder-blue trimline phone on the nightstand next to my head ringing, yanking me out of the dream. My body clock said it was far too early to be awake and when I opened my eyes, the room was still dark. *What time is it?* Five twenty-two AM. *Wrong number.* Grope for the receiver, knock it off the stand and drag it back by the cord. I closed my eyes again, prepared to go back to sleep as soon as the wrong number was confirmed.

"Hello?" My voice was sleep-drenched and irritated.

"Hello there," said a man's voice, tender, almost familiar.

"Hello?" I repeated, confused. I still thought it was a wrong number.

"Pattie? Is that you?"

"Yeah - who's -" *uh-oh*. As soon as I said it, I knew who it was, that guy from the Restola, what, six - eight weeks ago? I had forgotten him as soon as he left, I hadn't given him a single thought since, why would he be calling me now? Did I remember giving him my phone number? "Duane? Is that you?"

I could almost feel him beaming through the phone. "Yup!" he said with enthusiasm. "I'm out here at Bandy's, whyn't you come on out and we'll get some breakfast?"

"You're out where?"

"Bandy's! That place where you work?"

"Oh... no one calls it that."

"Why not?"

"Huh? I don't know!" I was testy, wished he would get to the point so I could hang up and go back to sleep.

"Well, uh, anyway, I'm out here where you work, at a phone booth and I just got here, I been drivin' for three days straight just t' be here - I been dyin' t' see you for two months now and I thought you could come out -"

"Duane, it's five-thirty in the morning."

"Come get me, darlin'," he said, almost crying. The desperate plea in his tone gave me no choice but to say *okay* and hang up.

Why did I do that? *Where did he come from?* What was *wrong* with me - I thought I was doing better with that.... I dragged myself out of bed, dragged myself into baggy sweats, blindly brushed my hair and dragged myself out of the sleeping house without brushing my teeth. Tiptoed past my snoring father, passed out in the living room chair. Why was I doing this - because he said he drove three straight days just to see me? Because I still can't say no, like an adult woman?

I blew on my frozen fingers while sitting in my cold car, waiting for the engine to warm up. Staring in the rearview mirror, watching clouds of steam billow out of the tailpipe, my mind was blank. I decided to ignore what I was doing, pretend this was dream. I could do that. I never saw this time of day, that alone felt unreal enough to be a dream. The drone of the engine and my lack of sleep was hypnotic, until I caught myself dropping off and shook my head back into focus. I resolved to do nothing, to be nothing, to give nothing. I couldn't think about it, I didn't have the strength, much less the wakefulness to take credible stock. I would be what I had never been before: resolved.

The car drove itself to the Restola in the misty predawn. I pulled into the parking lot, in front of the enormous front doors of the Restola and there he was. He groaned like an old man, dragged his bony frame off a bench and limped toward me with outstretched arms and a huge grin. Did he have that limp before? I let him have a reserved, sisterly hug, just a brief second, then stepped back and folded my arms in front of me. He smelled of old, sour sweat and a lot of cigarettes, his wild hair jutted out from under the same grimy cap and he had not shaved. He looked even older than I remembered, as if he had not slept since the last time he was here. If I had been a little more with-it, I would have thought to review what I did remember about him, if anything. We stood and faced each other for an awkward second, he so bleary-eyed he could barely manage to hold his smile, me at a complete loss at waking up and finding myself here, now, with *him?*

"Let's go in and have some breakfast," he said, motioning toward the coffee shop inside the Restola.

"Uh, okay, but not there. The food's not that good and it's expensive." Not to mention we could run into someone to whom I was related. It was a little after six. Probably an okay time to go in there, it was about an hour and a half before my mother and Lula would show up for their pre-work coffee-and-bitch session, but you could never be too careful with those two.

"You're in charge," he said, limping around the car and getting in the passenger seat as if he belonged there. I shrugged and got in. Fine, I would have breakfast with him. I could do that. I drove us back to Selma's Waffles, where we had breakfast last time, two months ago.

"It sure is great t' be back here with you," he said. His voice was so tired that he sounded as if he was admitting a defeat rather than being reunited with someone he was glad to see.

"Hmm." Wary, I tried to look too busy driving to say any more. It was his idea to show up out of nowhere, his idea to drag me out of bed in the middle of the night, it was up to him to do the talking.

He fidgeted with his cigarette, took off his cap and tried to run his fingers through his snarled hair. "Now I wish I'd stopped and got a shower and shave first, 'fore I called you," he said. He sounded confident when he called me, but my less than hearty greeting had taken some of that away from him. "You must think I'm a real pig."

"No," feeble, not knowing what else to say. Wonderful, he was making me uncomfortable already.

He sneezed violently into a grimy hanky and let out a long, horrible smoker's cough, cleared his throat and lit another cigarette. He cracked the window for ventilation and looked nervous while he smoked. "Lookit you, you're sleepy. I'm an asshole for wakin' you up like that, and expectin' you t' be happy t' see me. Thank you for comin' down here, darlin', I really appreciate it."

"Um, okay...." *Stop calling me "darlin".*

"That's somethin,' I guess, you comin' down here at all." He took a drag off his cigarette, rattled out another long cough, careful to point it away from me. "You work late last night?"

"Um, no... I was at a party."

"What kind of party?"

I shrugged, catching a slight sharpness in his hoarse voice. Or maybe it was my imagination. "Just a party."

He didn't pursue it. I stopped at a red light, drumming my fingers on the wheel to get the light to turn green. Taking advantage of his silence, I turned on the radio, loud enough to compete with any attempt at conversation but not loud enough to be accused of being deliberate. He started to say something, realized he wasn't being heard and turned it off. "D' you mind if we turn that off for now? I kinda got a little headache right now."

I shrugged again without answering. The light turned green and I pulled out, busying myself with shifting gears. Selma's came up on the right, its plain-lettered sign looming out from behind a rare weeping willow. How weird, I thought, Selma's Waffles was older than I was and this was only the second time in my life I had been here. My parents were never much for taking the family out to breakfast. The parking lot was full of puddles, testifying to more rain than I remembered last night.

Selma's had the same tired, overlit look of restaurants that never close. Plaid-shirted locals sat at the counter, read newspapers, drank muddy coffee and discussed life with the worn-out waitresses and each other before going off to their grease pit jobs. I felt so out of place, used to the slick and sanitized Restola. Duane looked right at home, the product of places like this.

Why am I here? It was a useless question. I slid into a worn red leatherette booth and nodded yes to the coffee proffered by the waitress with the gray-blonde beehive. Her eyeliner was crinkled and her red ruffled uniform revealed a little too much supp-hose. Or was this a dream? More likely, I was just trying to fool myself. *Is it working yet?*

I ordered toast with my coffee, the only thing my still sleeping and half-hungover stomach could handle. He got the hearty appetite special: eggs over easy, bacon, sausage, pancakes, potatoes and toast. "I didn't stop t' eat last night, I was in such a hurry t' get here, y' know. Seems the closer I got the harder I had t' drive and I just didn't wanna waste any time."

I said nothing, sipping my coffee. An hour ago, I was sound asleep and everything was normal and he didn't even exist. If I was so sure it was a wrong number, why did I answer the phone? I wouldn't make that mistake again. *Maybe I should get an answering machine before I start saving for the leather jacket.*

"I woulda got back sooner," he said, "but I hit a moose up in Vermont and broke my leg."

I almost choked on my coffee. *"What?"*

The waitress brought our food and he waited until she was gone to answer. He swirled the undercooked eggs around his plate, mixing them with the hash browns, shoveled a dripping forkful into his mouth. "I was takin' a load up there and a goddamn moose jumped in front of me and I ran right into it, mangled my grill and broke my leg."

"On a *moose?*"

"Yup."

"How do you break your leg like that on a *moose?*"

"You ever seen a moose? I mean, a real live moose, in person?"

I had to think about this for a minute. "No."

"Well, they're bigger than you think," he said, as if speaking to a wondering child.

I had trouble picturing it, but he insisted that's what happened. "I was stuck up there for two whole months practically - two weeks in the hospital, rest of the time sittin' a motel room, waitin' for the rig t' be fixed and watchin' it snow for six goddamn weeks all by myself."

"How come you had to stay in the hospital? I thought they just put a cast on it and gave you crutches and send you home."

"Nope," he said with finality, taking a bite of syrup-soaked pancake.

Whatever. "What about your family?"

"What about 'em?"

"Well, didn't they know you were in the hospital?"

He shrugged. "What could they do about it?"

"Well - they didn't come to visit you or nothing?" I had only gone to see my father once when he was in the hospital, and he was only a fifteen-minute bus ride away. I was overwhelmed with sentiment for my father and an embarrassing urge to cry, but I bit it back lest Duane think I was crying for him.

He took a few moments from his busy meal to sit back and let out a body-heaving sneeze that was startling in its intensity. He blew his nose into the same smutty hanky, replacing it in his back pocket. *Remind me not to slide over that way on my way out.* Leaning over his plate, he shook his head at the food, coughed and cleared his throat. "Must be gettin' a cold," he said.

"Hmm," uninterested and unsympathetic. I spread a little strawberry jam on the last bite of my toast and put it in my mouth, licked the butter remnants from my thumb and forefinger.

"What d' you wanna do after breakfast?" he said.

"Huh? Uh... I don't know." Why did I think breakfast would be it and then he would be gone? I could think of a dozen reasons why I couldn't spend any more time with him, but was unable to voice a single one. This was unfair. I couldn't think, he had me off guard ever since the phone rang.

He laughed at me. "Well, this is your territory. You're the only one here knows what there is t' do around here."

Involuntarily, I rolled my eyes. He looked so frail and unhealthy, and it made me all the more uncomfortable. He came all this way to see me, and I felt bad about hurting his feelings. It was flattering, regardless of my feelings toward him. No one had ever gone to that much trouble for me before and I couldn't bring myself to send him away thinking I was a bitch. I couldn't stand the thought of being described that way, to complete strangers all over the country, becoming part of Trucker Lore as that rude bitch back in Wattlesburg. What if I wanted to be famous for something else one day? There would always be that core group of people out there who knew about the way I treated this one guy and could say *oh her, I hear she's a real bitch.*

It was starting to come back to me, some of the things we talked about, or rather, things he talked about. There was something about a family history of suicidal tendencies and I was afraid if I turned him down, he would start talking about that again. How much did I tell him? I didn't remember saying much, and knew I hadn't told him about Steve.

Wherever we went after breakfast, it would have to be a safe place, where we wouldn't run into anyone I knew. There weren't that many choices around town. At least the choice was up to me. I could rule out anything that might lead him to think he was being given an invitation of any kind. Someplace public, if that was possible. I would be doing the driving, that gave me that much control, however tenuous.

He picked up the check and slid out of the booth. I downed the rest of my coffee and followed him to the cash register, remembering to slide out of the opposite side. This time I had no guilt about letting him pay: he appeared out of nowhere and demanded re-entry into my life at five-thirty in the morning, he could damn well pay for breakfast.

SIXTEEN

Morning had reached full light when we left the restaurant. The bright sun reflected the frozen winter heat from every surface, as if the morning dew had melted and hardened into varnish. It hit me in the head like a jackhammer. I shielded my eyes with my hand, but tiny razor-sharp beams cut between my fingers, each one creating a tiny headache of its own where it hit my face and forehead. The harsh sunlight was unkind to Duane, separating and magnifying every flaw, then rejoining the pieces into an exaggerated caricature of a man beaten down, old before his time. I shrank as far behind my hand as I could, hiding my face from the same fractious illumination. It was the same thing with my looks as with my disposition - I didn't want to be remembered and described as ugly, either.

"Oh, 'fore we go wherever we're goin'," he said when we were in the car, "I need t' stop and see if I can get a motel room there at the truck stop."

Motel? The word was a jolt. Was this a direct implication that he thought we might sleep together? I stared straight ahead at the road, gripped the wheel with both hands and tried to remain collected while acting as if I didn't catch the hint. To my surprise, he acted as if he hadn't dropped it. He wasn't even looking at me, fumbling in his pockets for a light for the cigarette hanging from his thin, chapped lips. He coughed hideously without dislodging the cigarette, about as unattractive a sight as I could imagine at the moment. *There is NO WAY, no way no way no way.*

The absoluteness of my resolve made me feel safe again, giving me such a sense of relief that I almost felt as if this whole thing was already over. It didn't matter where I took him, the moment he tried anything, I could wave bye-bye, absolved of any guilt for being rude. Even the law was on my side and for the first time, I was grateful to be only seventeen.

I kept quiet on the short drive back to the Restola, lest anything I said be twisted to mean I wanted to sleep with him. When I pulled up to the motel, I announced that I would wait in the car and to my surprise, he didn't argue.

Alone at last, I let out my deepest breath and rubbed my tired eyes. *What time is it...* seven-fifteen. Almost eleven hours before I could go to work. I could have fallen asleep, right there in my car seat, so I sat up and forced my eyes to stay open. The Restola sat across the parking lot to the west, quiet in the early morning but for a few early-rising elders. I had never seen it from this angle, from the motel end. I missed it, as if being there on the motel side removed me somehow. A pair of ravens swooped down on a scattering of crumpled burger wrappers, shredding and picking at the remains. They were repulsive, with their nasty beaks always into something dead and putrid. Everything was repulsive to me at that moment. Duane came out of the motel office wearing an absent, tired expression, got in, and reported he was all set.

What does that mean, was my sour thought. I had no intention of asking and inviting an unpleasant answer. Still he showed no more signs that he expected me to sleep with him and that was a relief. But from some dark and putrid part of my mind came the thought, *why not?* Was I not pretty, charming, sexy.... *Come on!* Throw that one out with the trash. I could hate myself for it later. *Why am I such a headcase?*

Now was the time to decide what to do with him. Automatically, I headed back to the reservoir. It was public enough to be safe but not public enough to be seen, if I was careful. He liked it well enough last time, he wouldn't care. It was boring up there without getting drunk, but that was one more thing I was not going to do with him. I didn't get drunk twice in a row. *What time is it?* Seven forty-five. Jesus, would this day never end?

"Can we stop at the store or somethin'?" he said, breaking the uncomfortable silence.

"Why?" Suspicious. "What do you need?"

"Just somethin' t' drink." He caught my suspicion and answered it with quizzical defensiveness, unsure how my suspicion applied to him.

Fine. There was a minimart on the way out of town. I pulled in, again saying I would wait in the car.

"Come on in with me," he said in a hurt tone. "You act like you don't even wanna be seen with me."

Bingo. Then I felt bad for my insensitivity. I was showing too much of myself. I wasn't trying to hurt his feelings, not unless he got out of line, and I wanted to avoid any depressing conversation. Appearances were important on both sides, so I got out and followed him inside.

Right there at the register, handing crumpled bills to a young clerk for a six-pack was Harvey O'Neill, one of my father's drinking buddies. Harvey looked like he had not slept or bathed in days. He reminded me of how my dad looked in the hospital, with his greasy black hair hanging in his yellow face and his wrinkled clothes hung with the ennui of the addicted. Harvey's red eyes were bulging out of their sockets, flicking from side to side with a vacant paranoia that meant he had been tweaking again. I tried to hide behind Duane without looking like I was hiding, but Harvey didn't see me. Even if he had, the possibilities of him remembering to tell my dad about it were slim and wasted.

Duane got a six-pack from the cooler, picked out a few bags of chips, turning the bags upside down to measure the contents, then moved to the sweets. He grabbed a couple two-packs of cupcakes, then it was back to the cooler for a six-pack of diet Pepsi. At the register, he added some Slim Jims and two packs of cigarettes. Overall, I'd say it was a disgusting combination. I hovered behind him, trying to be invisible, watching the door while he paid for everything. The only thing that looked remotely appetizing was the Pepsi. That toast was sitting on my stomach like a rock and the sight of the jerky sitting next to the cigarettes and the cupcakes made my stomach heave.

He gave me an unreadable smile on the way out. "Whaddaya think of that?"

"Huh?" Nervous laugh, clueless as to the meaning of his question. "I don't know."

He laughed at me again, happily hawked and spit on the asphalt. I looked away, pretending not to see, unsure how to react to the things he said and did.

The seatbelt buzzer howled when I started the car, but I refused to buckle up. It was one of my tiny unseen rebellions, one of the little secret things I did to tell myself that deep down, I really wasn't part of the herd. Dutiful Duane buckled himself in and cost himself a point he could ill afford to lose. I put on my sunglasses and drove up into the hills to the reservoir, past the boat launch where we stopped two months ago, past the spot where Frankie, Elvia and I got drunk the night he left. I hated Frankie anew; in my mind he was tied up with this whole situation and that gave me one more person to blame besides myself. Because of Duane, I had to ask a favor of Frankie, which gave Frankie the opportunity to tell lies about me. I was sick of the way these things turned out, and there I was again in another *situation*, just more of the same tired old bullshit.

Around the south side of the reservoir, I found a spot that was deserted but not too secluded, within sight of a couple of boats with fishing poles dangling in the water. It was a short walk down the slope to the water's edge and I could still see my car parked on the side of the road, a beacon in case he should decide to murder me. I left the blanket in the trunk, he would have to sit in the dirt. It didn't matter that I would be doing the same, it was just another idea I didn't want to give him.

We sat a few feet back from the water on the small crescent-shaped beach. The lake sat in apathy between the brown hills, reflected in the cloudy water. Duane pulled a beer out of the bag of groceries, then a Pepsi. "This is what you like, right?"

"Yeah, thanks." I was touched that he remembered what I liked to drink, then thought it was funny that he waited until now to confirm it, rather than asking me in the store. I sipped my soda, felt the little bubbles fizzing in my stomach and bringing it under control. The sun had risen over the hilltops and the corrosive bright light beat into my head despite my shades. It was already getting warmer than I expected it would be. I pushed my sweater sleeves up to my elbows, crossed my arms over my knees and wished I was at home, asleep.

"It sure is peaceful up here," he said, dreamy.

Oh? I never noticed. Peace, here? I looked around, but I didn't see peaceful. All I saw was drought, choking brown dusty drought.

"What're they catchin' out there?" he said.

"I don't know. Nobody I know fishes." His question startled me, I was lost in my own thoughts and had forgotten him again. Again, I felt bad for him. He remembered the Pepsi, least I could do was be civil to him.

"Nobody? That's a damn shame. Here you got this nice lake and no one fishes it."

"I didn't say *nobody*, I said no one I know. Those people are fishing," indicating the two boats on the lake.

"Yeah, but that's not very many. Figure a lake this size would have a lot more people on it."

"Well, lots of people gotta work. It's Tuesday, you know."

"That's true. I kinda lose track of what normal people do, 'cause I just drive when I have to and take a day off when I can, like today, which ain't too often."

"A lot of people come here to jetski, too."

He curled his lip. "You like doin' that?"

I shrugged my shoulders. "Never tried it before."

"Well, you wouldn't like it. Noisy as hell, scares the fish, just kills all the peace and quiet."

Peace and quiet. It was quiet, I guess. I stared out across the lake, wished I could vow to try jetskiing at the first available opportunity, but I could foresee none. Who the hell did he think he was, telling me what I wouldn't like? My hostility was creeping back. My end of this inane conversation was over. We sat in silence for a while, me withdrawn and unconcerned, he silent by habit of solitude. Time went by and my hostility receded. I was still reluctant to be outright rude, so I let myself be drawn back in by his harmless questions about my daily life.

"I just love sittin' by the water, don't you?" he said. "It's so restful. You wouldn't believe how keyed-up you get, humped over a steerin' wheel all day and night, tryin' t' keep your eyes open, starin' at the road passin' under your wheels, stayin' awake for days 'cause everyone expects you t' make a four-day run in three - that's 'sposed t' be illegal, but they all do it anyway - tryin' t' keep your logbooks lookin' legal so D.O.T. don't ground you, watchin' every dollar you make go right back out twice as fast as you made it.... Person gets pretty keyed up." He lit a cigarette and hacked out a cloud of smoke. "Don't you think?"

"Yeah, I bet. I mean, I never drove a truck before."

"No, I know that, silly. I mean, don't you love sittin' by the water?"

"I don't know, I guess. I don't come up here much. I mean, I come up here sometimes, but I never really look at the water, I guess."

"Well, you don't fish, you don't jetski, you don't look at the water, what do you do up here?"

Another shrug. "Hang out with my friends."

He didn't say anything and I thought he was disappointed in me. "I been to the ocean a couple of times, I like that better," I said.

"I went deep-sea fishin' once, down in the Gulf, and I got sick as hell," he said.

"At least the ocean's alive and moving, not like this. This just... *sits* there. It's boring."

"Well, maybe we can go see the ocean sometime."

"Hmm." *I don't think so.* I sipped my warm soda and tried to think of a way to change the subject. He crushed his empty beer can, setting it in the dirt in front of him. He took the last drag off his cigarette and stubbed it out next to the can, leaving the butt sticking up in the air like a weathered bone fragment poking out of the desert. He drank in the quiet, tried to will the fatigue from his bones by wearing a restful expression. His eyes were very red and kind of jumpy. It was a little warm out but he was sweating like it was July, far more than the early spring sun justified. He looked so far beyond tired that he could pass out right there before me, but for those jumpy eyelids. He was waiting it out pretty calmly, he must have been well accustomed to the phases of the amphetamine moon.

I was revolted by Duane's choice of picnic foods earlier in the morning, but by nine o'clock, cupcakes and beef jerky were beginning to sound pretty good. I was hungry, but he paid for the food, so it wasn't my place to break it out. I could ask, but then someone might feel like I owed him something. He had to offer it to me or I couldn't eat it. One of the boats had moved off, leaving me with only one protector. *Bullshit, I am my own best protector.* It was a surprising thought, had I ever thought that of myself before? Was it anger at Duane for pushing himself back into my life or anger at myself for letting him? Both. Me. *Me.*

There were three crumpled beer cans and six cigarette butts lined up in front of him before he got hungry and opened the bag. The cans and butts looked like he was trying to spell out a message. Possibilities: *I drink too much beer after breakfast. Desperately seeking a smoky death. Defeat is my middle name.*

"Hungry?" He offered me a pack of cupcakes.

"Sure." Trying to sound indifferent, I accepted the cupcakes with a shrug that said I didn't care if I never saw food again.

He tore open a bag of chips and set them on the ground between us, offered me another soda and himself another beer. "I couldn't wait t' get outta that damn hospital up there. I was never so glad t' see a beer in my whole life. Hospital food's the worst there is, worse than truck stop food. They feed you this mushy, tasteless crap and don't give you enough of that even, and forget getting any kind of good coffee. I tried t' get the nurses t' sneak me a six-pack or somethin', but they never would. Maybe if I was better lookin'." He paused and looked at me, but got no reaction. "Even the ugly ones wouldn't help me out none and that's bad when you can't even get an ugly nurse t' feel sorry for you."

"Okay, now tell me again," I said through a mouthful of chocolate cupcake. "You hit a *moose* and broke your leg in your rig and you had to be in the hospital for two weeks? That doesn't make sense."

"Well, believe me, I wouldn't have stayed there a minute longer than I had to. I can't stand bein' closed up like that, dependin' on other people just t' get to the toilet. I woulda flew down here, but I didn't have the money. I had t' borrow money just t' get the rig fixed, that's why that took so long. You ever spend two weeks in a hospital bed?"

"No."

"Well, it's mighty goddamn boring." He drained his fourth beer, crushed the can and added it to the lineup. "Depressing. Same four walls every day, can't even get no rest 'cause folks are poppin' in and out all the time, day and night, lookin' you over and wakin' you up t' take your damn temperature and ask you how you feel. Stupidest goddamn question you can ask someone who's in the hospital. I mean, why would you even be in the hospital if you didn't feel like shit?"

Shrug. "I don't know."

"And that motel room wasn't much better. All cooped up, still couldn't walk right, lookin' out the same goddamn window every day, not makin' no money, missin' your loved ones. Might as well be back in the hospital. Don't cost as much t' stay in a motel as in the hospital, 'cept motels want their money up front. I had t' borrow money t' get the rig outta the shop, now that's one more I owe, 'cause I needed t' get back here."

"How come?"

"Huh?"

"How come you had to get back here?"

He drank the rest of his beer and stared into the empty can. "I came back here to get married."

I caught my breath. He wasn't here for me, *oh thank God.* It made sense now, he didn't want anything, he was hurting over a broken engagement and I was just someone to cry to. I felt intensely sorry for all my mean thoughts, now it was okay to be nice to him, because he didn't want anything. "What happened?" I said with sympathy, serious in my newfound role.

"Well...," he stammered, flushed with regret at his words, but seeing nowhere to go but forward. "Nuthin,' yet, I just opened my mouth 'fore I planned on. I was gonna spend the day, have a nice dinner and then ask you right, but I blew that."

Oh-my-God.... He was talking about *me*, he meant he thought he was here to marry *me*. *Marry* me! I didn't see that coming at all, *my God, what do I do?* The idea was so absurd that I wasn't sure if I heard him right and if I did, that he really meant what I thought he said. All I could do was stare at him with my mouth open, as if he had just announced he was from Mars. "What? Ask me *what?*"

"Ask you t' marry me," he said sadly, already prepared for the rejection that was coming.

"I - you don't even *know* me, how can you want to marry me - I mean, you spend a few hours with me and go off for two months, don't even call or *anything*, then just show up and think -"

"I'm sorry, darlin,' I didn't mean for it t' just come out like that. I mean, I just been so nervous, and so anxious, all I been thinkin' about the whole time since I left here was you -"

"But you didn't even call me!" *Listen to me*, assuming the role of wronged participant. But I didn't know how else to react, it was so one-sided that it made no sense.

"I know, and I should be ashamed, treatin' you bad like that and we ain't even married yet." He shook his head, afraid to look at me. "I'm just real bad about that kinda thing, I just hate talkin' on the phone. This ain't the way I wanted t' do it at all. I wanted t' sweep you off your feet, take you out for a nice dinner and ask you right, not just spit it out without you even bein' prepared for it, like some big shock and scare you off, like I just did."

"Well - how could I not be shocked? I mean...." I didn't know what I meant. It felt so very weird, another *situation* for which I had no experience, my first proposal, *marriage*. I tried to picture what he was proposing, *this man* as my husband, but I couldn't do it. It was supposed to be a two-choice question, but I never heard of anyone saying *no* to a marriage proposal, never seen it on TV, and I wasn't quite sure how to say it.

"I got my cousin Jimmy waitin' in a motel in Bakersfield for me t' call him t' come up and be my best man. I know I blew it, though." He turned and faced me, imploring. "Don't say nuthin' yet, please, I know what you're gonna say anyway, can't you just forget it? I promise I won't talk about it no more, I promise, okay?"

Still in shock, I stared at him like a surprised sheep. So many impossible thoughts ran through my head - me in little ruffled *I Love Lucy* aprons doing Suzy Homemaker things. Despite my exposure to the realities of married life - my mother didn't wear aprons - all I could picture was the Ozzie and Harriet experience. It was that improbable. The image deteriorated to one of myself locked in a lifeless little crackerbox house in a trashy neighborhood in a dead town, just like the one I lived in now. What do you say when a complete stranger asks you to marry him? Your very first marriage proposal, and it's a complete surprise, from someone you could never stand to have touching you, and he looked so pathetic, staring at the water with his twitchy, bloodshot eyes brimming with tears. I had forgotten about him, for God's sake. When he called this morning, it wasn't that I recognized his voice, it was just that he was the only person I'd ever known with that Missouri twang, so it was the first name that popped into my head (and out of my mouth). You hang out for a few hours with a guy who picks you up at work and then he thinks you're gonna *marry* him, marry *him*, you're seventeen years old and you've never been in love, real love, not teen-idol love. Whatever *real love* is, I wasn't going to find it with this guy and whatever else I didn't know about life, I knew I'd like a shot at that.

Poor Duane looked like he would break down if I said anything, so I didn't, hoping he would do the same. I saw no choice but to let it go as he asked. I could forget it. I didn't have to say *yes*, and I had already implied *no*.

"But I'd be honored," he said, "if you'd just have dinner with me tonight. I swear I'll be good, you don't even have t' worry about a thing."

"I can't, I gotta work." Huge relief, I almost forgot. The savior of Responsibility strikes again.

"Work?" His face fell, losing what little hope he might have gained if I had dinner with him. "Can't you get the night off or somethin'?"

"No, I can't, it's too late to switch with someone."

"Can't you call in sick or somethin'?"

"No! You call in sick too much and you get fired. I need my job." Haven't we had this conversation before?

He grinned. "That'd be okay, then you wouldn't have t' worry 'bout it no more. I'd take care of you." He saw me recoil and apologized again. "I'm sorry. I promise I won't do it no more. I'll be good from now on, I swear."

"I can't. I really have to go to work." I was already tired of this game.

"Okay. Can I at least come in and visit with you?"

"I'm not gonna be able to visit with you, I'll be working!"

"That's okay, I won't bother you. I'll just sit real quiet-like, out of the way while I read my newspaper and drink my coffee. Maybe if it gets slow for a bit, I can come up and say hi t' you real quick, that's all. I promise I won't bother you."

My head hurt. I looked away from him, down at the hard brown earth, dry now after last night's sprinkling. I would go crazy with him hanging around the restaurant. Maybe I could switch with someone in the back, *dammit,* that worked out so well last time. Fine, fine, he could come in a stay all night if he wanted to. I would simply stay as busy as possible. Tuesday wasn't usually a heavy traffic night, but maybe I'd get lucky and get several busloads of rowdy soccer kids or Japanese tourists or something. And, if he was too much of a pest, I could have the manager throw him out. "Fine," I said, trying to sound unenthusiastic without being rude.

He brightened a little, picked up his empty beer cans and put them in the grocery bag, as if he was packing up to leave. Might as well seize the opportunity while he was willing, so I stood up and fished out my car keys. He looked a little confused at first, but took the hint and picked up the rest of the uneaten junk food. I fiddled with the toys on my keyring while he took inventory: smokes, shades, lighter, brew.... He stood up too fast and gave himself a headrush, swaying on his feet, trying to get a grip on his skull. He had to light another cigarette before he was ready to follow me up to the car, limping and coughing all the way.

We were both quiet and withdrawn on the ride back. On his first visit, he had maintained a running monologue, revealing layers of his world as if he were peeling off his flesh piece by piece, standing before me as naked as a skeleton. Now I supposed he expected me to do the same, but I wasn't talking. Maybe he thought I was shy and if I got to know him, maybe I would start to like him. The only way to show himself was to *tell* me. I didn't think it was enough. It could never be enough.

The tension inside the car was thick, magnifying my fear that despite how careful and mature I thought I was being, I was heading into more than I could handle and I wasn't going to be able to control it. My fingernails dug themselves into the blue leather steering wheel cover, then I realized what I was doing and retracted them, rubbing the leather and mentally apologize to my car. The apology became a mantra, *sorry, Belinda, sorry, Belinda,* over and over so I didn't have to think about anything else.

By the time we get to the Restola, I was drained. I let him out in front of the motel without turning off the engine, said nothing and prayed he wouldn't give me another speech before he got out.

"I'll see you later," he said, with a lack of enthusiasm that made me hope he wouldn't show up. I hoped I got off easy this time, hoped this strange chapter of my life was closing. But I was wrong. He did come back.

SEVENTEEN

The house was empty when I get home, and I thanked God for the best thing that had happened to me all day. I was still hungry, but there was nothing in the refrigerator that was already prepared, and I was too tired to fix anything. Instead, I went to my room and got into bed. Knowing that Elvia would call, I unplugged the phone.

What a weird day, I concluded, rubbing my aching forehead and trying to get my eyes to close. I still couldn't see how he had come to his conclusions. No matter how you fit the pieces of our lives together, it still came out two different pictures. It was almost funny. Elvia would love it, in a vicious sort of way, but I thought I would have a hard time explaining any of it without her laughing at me too. She would want to know what I had to gain by stringing him along and I didn't know.... I couldn't even see where I had been stringing him along - he left, he disappeared, he came back - with marriage on his mind? How did that happen? Where did I do any stringing? I was uncomfortable with this train of thought and pushed it out of my head in favor of putting myself to sleep by reviewing what happened on my soaps the last time I watched - yesterday, was it?

home alone on another day, another time
our house is very different
with an open breezy feel that is lacking in reality
as if the walls have been replaced with thin white draperies
lilting in the air
mom and dad are away at work
and my mother has left me with a baking assignment
I grumble around the kitchen, drag bowls from the cupboard
and slop flour in them
not quite sure what I'm supposed to be making
glance out the window, catch sight of my brother coming to the back door

suddenly wary of him and forgetting he's supposed to be dead
I retreat from the windows to an angle where I can't be seen

he knocks, waits, knocks again
I skulk in the shadows and will him to go away
I don't want him to see how many bowls I'm using
he knocks again then leaves to sneak around and peek in the other windows
I don't think he's up to anything evil,
I just don't want him in the house right now
He moves around to the other side of the house
I follow from inside, darting into corners where I can't be seen
If I'm a stationary shadow, I'm invisible
a moving shadow will give me away

later the same day, my parents are home
the three of us sit in the living room
knitting
no sign of whatever I tried to bake
he walks in the door just like every day
is welcomed into the bosom of the family
as if he's never been dead
For the life of me, I can't think
why I ever wanted to hide from him

Later when I got to work, I was surprised to see Duane sitting in a corner booth, facing the counter, drinking coffee and reading the newspaper. He looked up, gave me a discreet wave, then went back to his paper. There was no reason I should be surprised, but I was. Wasn't he embarrassed?

He nursed his coffee until the dinner rush was over, then came up to order his own dinner. He grinned at me and I smiled awkwardly back, no more than I would give any other stranger. But this one was different, as much as I didn't want him to be. This one was mine. And he looked like hell. "Are you alright?" I blurted out before I could think.

He sagged with relief, now he didn't have to buck up for me anymore. "No, darlin,' I'm not. When you dropped me off earlier, I forgot I left my gear in the rig which was parked way on the other side and I had t' walk all the way across that parking lot and back with my rear end draggin' 'bout three feet behind me. And all the time I'm shiverin' like it's freezin' out, when I should be sweatin' like crazy. That ain't a good sign, y' know."

"Why not?"

"Means I'm sick, and I got no time for that shit." He shook his head, leaned on the counter. "No time for that shit. By the time I got back up t' my room, I had the cold sweats and the spins. I just collapsed on my bed without even takin' my boots off and watched the ceiling spin. And my head's ringin' from the sound of the road, it just roars in my head all the time. All the time, no matter where I am. Y' know what I wonder sometimes?"

"What?" I was feeling very sorry for him again. It was a short step from sorry to guilty, and I would have to watch my footing.

"I wonder if the day ever comes when I can get off the road, will I still hear that drone in my head for the rest of my life, day and night?"

I didn't know what to say to that, so I just shrugged. I wanted to say something kind and soothing but I didn't have the words, and I didn't want him to misconstrue anything I did say.

He let out a cough so miserable that it made my own chest hurt. "Y' know, my whole body's just poundin' right along with this hammer beatin' down on my head." He made pounding motions over his head with his fist.

"I'm sorry." *How awful it must be to be you.*

"But no way I could sleep, so I forced myself t' get up and come down here and do some laundry and I nearly choked t' death on that soap powder, y' know how it gets in the back of your throat if you're not careful when you're pourin' it, you can't even breathe around that stuff without chokin' on it, and I already got a bad cough t' start with, so that didn't help, either."

I almost laughed, then realized he wasn't making a joke. "Well - I'm sorry. Do you want some food?" That much I could offer. Just doing my job.

"I thought I did when I came up here, but now I ain't so sure."

"Well -" I wanted to say, *why don't you just go back and go to bed,* but I didn't want to use the word *bed* or *sleep* or anything so related.

"I'll just have some more coffee and go back and sit down. I'll be alright, don't worry 'bout it."

His illness made me feel more obligated not to hurt or upset him. The helpless state he was showing frightened me anew - you don't abandon someone who is down that low. I tried my best to look as busy as possible, but it was tough once the dinner rush was over. The struggle was relieved by the occasional worn-down traveler, all of whom seemed to have colds, handing me their money with the same shaky, coughed-on hands. Few looked as desperate as Duane, but I saw his face on every one. Was it that tough and lonely on the road? There must be countless girls like me, in places like this, all over America, handing food to the sick and the lonely coming in off the road. I felt sorry for all of them and sorrier for Duane, but I was afraid of being too friendly for fear they would misinterpret, the way Duane had.

I stole momentary glances at him, huddled in his back corner booth with his paper, trying to draw himself in as close as possible to keep from shivering. Why wasn't he wearing a jacket? He didn't seem to have the energy to bother me, and there was something heartrending about him, sitting there all alone. There was no fun in his life, no relief from the road. How many of these travelers could tell the same story? What is it in people that drives them to spend their lives in constant transit, never reaching or finding a final destination or place where they can say *there*, and drop their burdens?

He wasn't a bad guy, he was actually very nice, unattractive though he was. But with all he told me, how could he expect anyone to marry into such a bleak existence? Would it look this bleak if I loved him? I was not equipped to alleviate his pain. Marrying him would be to sentence myself to the same soul-consuming loneliness, couldn't he see that?

I didn't know why I kept trying on his life, like a blouse I was thinking of buying. I was not going to marry him. He was not the only one with troubles. My life had not been easy, either, and I resented him for making me feel sorry for him when he knew nothing about me. Still, the intensity of his experience was different from my own and it made an absorbing focus for my curiosity and my imagination. Every once in a while, I heard him sneeze and cough over in his corner booth and watched him blow his nose into the same dirty hanky, a lost waif with no one to care about him. The fact that his plight didn't move me enough to be *The One* just added to the pity. I saw a man on borrowed time, with burdens so crushing that he was only walking around by sheer force of will. Remember what he said about suicide the last time he was here? With such despair, I wondered why he didn't. I felt myself on a tightrope, one false step and it was him who went down without a net.

* * *

Around midnight, when business had trickled down to nearly nothing, he came back for more coffee. Because he looked straight at me, I greeted him, trying to be polite but not overly concerned.

"Things look pretty slow around here," he whispered, "think maybe they'll let you off a little early?"

No. "I don't think so." He was making me nervous again. I glanced backward at the shift leader loitering nearby, hoping he hadn't heard that. "They don't like us to ask stuff like that."

"How come? Nuthin's goin' on here right now."

"Not right now, but things can change. We're supposed to work certain hours and I don't want to get in trouble."

"Okay, that's fine, don't worry 'bout it. I'll just sit back down and wait like a good boy. It's kinda nice to watch you work, you work real hard, and I know you're not doin' it just to impress me. My instincts were right about you, I like that."

I looked away and wished he would sit down like he promised, but he didn't move. He sagged against the counter and rubbed his forehead. "Y' know, I think I might be able to go to sleep soon. Might even be tonight."

"Not with all that coffee you're drinking."

"Oh no, darlin', I was weaned on coffee, I'm immune to it. It's like water t' me. You know what - I'm goin' to the store over there," he pointed back toward the lobby, "and get some beer and some pills. D' you want somethin' t' drink too? I don't even know what you like to drink, 'cept Pepsi."

"I don't know if I can -"

"Oh, come on," he wailed, much louder than he needed to. "I ain't gonna hurt you, you oughta know that by now, darlin'. I'm tired and sick, and I just want you t' have one drink with me, 'fore I try and go to sleep. You can do that much, can't you?"

"Okay, okay," I acquiesced just to get him to quiet down.

"There, that wasn't so hard, was it? So what do you want t' drink?"

"Um - uh, how about Kahlua and cream?" I couldn't get drunk on that.

"Say *what?*"

"Kahlua and cream. Coffee liqueur and half-and-half over ice. It's really good."

"Well, I never heard of it, but I'll see if they got it."

"Thanks."

"Okay. I'll see you out there when you're through here." He waved his thumb at the lobby and went away, laughing to himself about Kahlua and cream.

Okay... so we would have a drink together. I snickered at the sight of him mumbling to himself and wondered if I should be worried about this, about him, alcohol, worried. I could see him when he came out of the minimart with a bag in his arms and sat on the circular plastic bench in the middle of the lobby, looking at his watch. He caught me looking at him, held up two hands to signal how much time I had left to work. All I could do was slink away to look busy for the rest of my shift. At two o'clock, I put on my sweater over my uniform and joined him in the lobby, trying to check around for people I knew without being too obvious about it.

"Hey," he stood and greeted me, cradling his bag. "Where we goin'?"

"Uh - go?" I stammer. "I don't know." *Not back to the lake.*

"Then let's just go up to the room. It's right here."

I hesitated at his suggestion, kicked myself for not thinking of this before, for having to say *I don't know.* It didn't even occur to me. There was no place to go, unless I could get him to just sit in the car, but it was too cold out there and he was sick, remember? Sick made him harmless, right, it would be okay, he would be fine, he'd been fine so far, he was just a little strange, that's all.

The parking lot was almost empty, but for the fringe of big rigs at the lower end. His must be among them. A chilly wind sliced down from the hills, skimmed across the expanse of parking lot like a herd of cold-fingered witches, leaving a frigid wake in the flat emptiness of the endless valley. The wind cut through me as if I was naked, and I pulled my sweater across my chest, folded my arms and tensed all of my muscles against the cold. Like the rape whistle, it was a hopeless defense. I insisted on driving across the parking lot instead of walking to the motel, so my car would be right there in case I had to get out in a hurry.

On the short drive across the deserted lot, I could feel the entire town watching me go into a motel with this person, laughing at me, thinking they knew what I was up to, passing judgement... but what could I do about it? I started this, or I let it get started, and I had to go through with it. I could hate myself for it later. Just a drink. Someday, I was going to learn... Let this teach me, I thought to myself.

Climbing up the stairs to his room did little to warm me. The wind whipped up as soon as we started up the pebbled cement steps, forcing the cold in through my very pores. In his cramped room, dominated by the queen-size bed, I sat in an uncomfortable chair with scratched-up wooden arms and tried to pretend the bed was not there, that this was not a motel room, that I was not in a motel room with a man. He emptied the bag on the mirrored dresser: a six-pack of beer, a small bottle of Kahlua, a pint of half-and-half, two packs of cigarettes and a packet of cold pills. Using a bone-handled pocket knife, he opened the pills, downed two and lit a cigarette to wash them down.

"You need ice for this stuff, too, right?"

"Uh-huh."

"Be right back, then," he said and limped out with a plastic ice bucket in one hand, coughing into the other through his cigarette.

I turned on the TV and asked myself why I was there. It was a stupid question not to be able to answer. *Who would ever know....* Because he bought Kahlua for me, I thought I should drink some of it, or his feelings would be hurt. Kahlua is expensive. Because I was trapped in my own game, because I'd never experienced having a man in love with me and willing to do whatever I wanted, and because he once - twice? - used the word *suicide* and he might be safer with me here than with me gone? I couldn't be so stupid as to get hooked in by someone who was dangerous, that just couldn't be. *It'll be fine, it'll be fine, it'll be fine.*

Where the hell is he? I was uncomfortable enough with my own thoughts to wish he would get back. One drink, and I was outta there.... The movie I found on TV broke for commercial and there was the Cal Worthington music. It droned on and on, made me think of my mother and laugh, then cut abruptly to an ad for truck driver school.. *Where the hell is he?* Twenty minutes later, he returned, laughing humorlessly at himself for getting lost.

"Lost?" I was irritated. "How can you get lost in a place like this?"

"Well, it's pretty damn easy when you been drivin' for days without sleep and your brains are fried. Besides, I ain't that smart t' begin with, so it's even easier for me."

Now I felt bad for making him say he was stupid. He brought a cellophane-wrapped plastic cup from the bathroom and unwrapped it, dropping the cellophane on the dresser next to the empty grocery bag.

"Okay," he said when he had filled the cup with ice. "What do I do next?"

"Put in this much Kahlua," I held up three fingers, "and the rest half-and-half."

"How come they don't just call it Kahlua and half-and-half?"

I shrugged my shoulders, seeing no point in answering that. He picked up the brownish mixture and studied it, watching the two liquids swirl and separate. "Looks like somethin' that'll make you sick 'fore it makes you drunk. It needs stirring, huh?"

"Oh, I can just kinda shake it around." I reached for the glass, but he picked up his sunglasses and stuck a bow in the drink to stir it. "No! Don't use that," I cried, but it was too late. *Ick*. He agitated my drink with the crusty bow, dissolving God-knows-what into it. I thought I would be sick.

Ignoring my protest, he picked it up and studied it again, looking satisfied. "Mind if I have a little sip, just t' see what it tastes like?"

"Go ahead." *Have the whole damn thing.*

He took a small taste and made a face. "Tastes like a Brandy Alexander, without the brandy. Why don't you just drink those?"

"Because I like these." I took my drink and looked at it with distaste. At least, I used to like them.

"How is it?"

I took as small a taste as possible. "It's fine." *Gross.*

He looked pleased with himself and his new Pattie-pleasing skill. In his fantasy, he would make me a Kahlua and half-and-half every night after dinner. "Look what I got for us," he said, rustling in a bag and pulling out two western shirts, still folded up in their plastic wrappers.

"What are those?"

"Shirts. See? His and hers." He was excited, pulling the wrappers off and handing one to me. He unfolded his and held it up to his chest. "See? Ain't they pretty?"

Oh God, I'd seen those things on two identically dressed manikins in the window of the western store where my mom works. Life-size Ken and Barbie dolls wearing these very same matching orange and black plaid shirts with pearl snaps and fancy stitching on black yokes and cuffs. Thank God he didn't also get the matching cowboy hats.

"I thought they'd be nice t' wear out dancin' or somethin'."

"Dancing?"

"Yeah! Don't you think? Maybe if there's a cowboy bar 'round here, or somethin', you know how to two-step?"

"No."

"Well, I can teach you. It's easy and I can prob'ly teach you."

"But there's no place like that around here."

"Don't you like 'em?" He sounded wounded. Although one of the shirts would be worn by him, both were a gift to me.

I stared at the shirt, trying to like it. I would never wear something like this. Nobody wore this stuff, except people like him. "No, I like it. It's really nice. Thanks."

He beamed, satisfied, and excused himself to the bathroom. I flipped channels on the TV until I found an old black and white monster movie, still holding the shirt. I cringed at the thought that my own mother might have sold him those stupid shirts. I had a momentary panic at the thought of Duane talking to my mother, telling her God-knows-what, about me. Had I told him my mother worked there? I hoped not, I wouldn't have done that, but I couldn't remember. I still didn't remember giving him my phone number. If he had never gone in there, I could be sure I had not told him, but the possibility made me doubt myself.

He wouldn't just blurt out his unreal plans to some strange woman selling him shirts, mention me by name? Would he? Look at all he dumped on me, at my work. As chatty as he was, he and my mother could not fail to discover each other if he hung around much longer, if they hadn't already. I could deny everything if I had to. *Honest, Mom, I don't know, he's just some guy who keeps coming in at work and bugging me. That's my story and I'm sticking to it.*

There was a crash in the bathroom, a large dull thud like a piece of furniture hitting the ground. I waited a few seconds, but didn't hear anything else, so I set the shirt on the chair, stood and listened at the bathroom door. Still nothing. I turned off the TV - nothing. Timid, I knocked. "Duane, are you alright?"

Nothing. I knocked again, harder, and when he still didn't answer, I was scared. "Duane! Are you in there?"

I tried the knob; it was unlocked, but blocked. I shoved the door with my shoulder and pushed it open a few inches, enough to see his feet, just enough to see that he was lying on the floor. *Oh God, what if he's dead? What do I do? Is he old enough to have a heart attack?* I tried pushing the door open wider, but there was no more give. Then a deep snore wafted through the small opening and I jumped back, startled. *He's only sleeping.* I wanted to laugh, clapping my hand over my mouth to stifle a giggle fit and the picture of him, toppling off the throne and landing flat-cheeked against the tile with his pants around his ankles and snoring his head off, felled at last by post-amphetamine narcosis.

That was it for me. I picked up my purse and left, leaving the gift shirt on the chair. *What a jerk, passed out on the pot.* He was going to be so embarrassed when he woke up that he would never have the balls to call me or see me again.

EIGHTEEN

But he did call me again. When the phone rang at a quarter to four the same morning, I knew it was him. "I'm sorry, darlin'," his voice cried from my phone. "I sure know how t' show a lady an excitin' time, don't I? I'm sorry, I just been so tired and wantin' t' sleep so bad, but I didn't know it would come over me all of a sudden like that." He paused, waiting for my reassurance, but I said nothing. "I don't blame you for goin' home, I was just so disappointed when I woke up and you were gone." He paused again, but I said nothing, so he got to the point. "Why'nt you come on back now? Please?"

"*What?* Duane, it's four in the morning. I was *asleep.*"

"I know. Can't you come sleep over here?"

"No! I'm already asleep here. I gotta work until two in the morning and you called me at five-thirty yesterday and now I'm tired! I gotta get some sleep!"

"I know, I'm just as tired, prob'ly more, I bet. You can come and get some sleep over here. I swear to you you'll be safe, I won't try nuthin' funny, I'm just so tired and sick and I'd sleep so much better if I know you were here with me. Please!"

"If you're gonna be asleep anyway, you won't know if I'm there or not."

"Yes, I will! Please, darlin', I'm beggin' you. I can't get no more desperate than that. Can't you do one little thing for me?" There were tears in his voice, he was trying not to let it break but if he had to, he would. "I swear you won't have nuthin' t' worry about. I just want you t' come back and stay with me. Come on," he wheedled in his best hurt tone, until I said yes, just to shut him up and get him off the phone.

Instantly sorry for my assent, I lay there. I had done it again. What was *wrong* with me? What stopped me from saying *no* to an ill stranger who had my phone number and might kill himself? I could ignore him and go back to sleep, but he would just call back and keep calling until I went there. There was no changing the fact that he had my number, not at four in the morning. Why couldn't I just hang up on him? I wasn't responsible for his troubles. I wasn't responsible if he killed himself.

My list of things for which to hate myself grew and grew. I got up, dressed in heavy, impenetrable layers and drove back to the motel, wondering if he really would have cried if I had said no. I didn't want to find out. I couldn't believe he'd called me at all; wasn't he mortified when he woke up in the bathroom with his pants down? Did he think I didn't notice?

Despite his fervid assurances, I could still be strolling right into trouble. If so, that would make me stupid and I couldn't be that, not after all of this. Sick as he was, and annoyed as I was, I had trouble seeing any real threat and that made me feel safer, that was as alright as I could make it.

He answered the door fully dressed but for his shoes, which struck me as odd for someone on their way to bed. It also struck me that he could have answered the door in any state of undress and I shuddered, feeling too close to another brush with real trouble. Without a word, he closed the door behind me and got into bed without taking anything off. Awkward, I stood by the door, not sure what to do. He sneezed hard and blew his nose, then coughed until I was sure his lungs would explode right out of his throat. When he was finished, he moaned in agony and patted the other side of the bed, then turned over with his back to where I would lie.

"Come on and go back t' sleep. You're kinda cranky when you're tired. Turn off the light, huh?" He pulled the blankets over his head and said no more, already asleep.

I stood frozen, confused by a torrent of images this *situation* presented. I was getting into bed with a man in a motel room. A *strange* man who was giving me clothes and asking me to marry him, yet had sworn not to touch me if I got into bed with him. He was already snoring. I couldn't sleep here if I tried. He was curled into a tight mass on his edge of the bed, with his back to me, dead to the world. I took off my shoes and got in, all layers of clothes still on, curled myself into an even tighter wad and perched on the very edge of my side of the bed with my back to him. Every muscle in me was tensed on that metaphoric edge. I was aware of too much, it was overwhelming, his *presence* was huge and filled the bed, trying to take over. *I can't do this.* I got up and sat in the uncomfortable chair and thought about how this was not quite how I pictured it would be, the first time I spent the night with a man.

He snored and coughed his way through the night and most of the morning, until ten-thirty, when an uncontrollable coughing fit finally woke him all the way up. I was so stiff I could hardly get out of the chair. He looked as if he had aged another ten years overnight.

"Mornin' darlin'," he croaked. His cold was visibly and painfully worse and he was so hoarse he could barely talk. As soon as he tried to stand, he was gripped by another savage cough that sounded as if he would never catch his breath. He heaved and hacked in a frightening way, and when it was finally under control, he swung his legs out of the bed and lit a cigarette, coughing with the burning cigarette hanging from his lips.

I pulled the chair around to face away from him and sat to put on my shoes. My head and neck ached, as if a knife was jammed into the base of my skull and my butt hurt from the uncomfortable chair. I also had to pee, but I was too squeamish to do so in his bathroom.

"Gawd," he groaned, rubbing his unshaven neck while smoke curled out of his nostrils. "My throat feels like it's burnin' up."

"Yeah, no wonder, the way you smoke."

"Don't be mean t' me," he whined. "I'm sick. I need someone t' be nice t' me, not mean."

"Um, I gotta go." I picked up my purse, leaving the shirt, still draped over the chair where I left it last night.

"Hang on," he said, looking through his wallet. He found what he was looking for, picked up the phone and dialed.

Now what? I stood by the TV, uncomfortable and a little nauseous. How do you act the morning after *nothing?* I sat back down in the chair and wished I was home in my own bed, *alone* and sleeping, wished I had never answered the phone last night, yesterday morning, that he had gone into the Taco Bell instead of my place two months ago and hooked up with Darlene Kimball, with her plastic helmet hair and her grainy black mascara. Or, with Amy Robinette with her scrawny, colorless hair, her pudgy face and little sausage fingers. Duane and Amy would have been perfect for each other. Anyone but me.

Elvia would be wondering what had happened to me. I hadn't talked to her since Maggie's party and I would have to think of something to tell her. Certainly not the truth. I could never explain this to Elvia, who had no trouble saying *no* to anyone, for anything. Elvia had no trouble saying *yes* either, and that would always be the difference between her and me. I almost wished he would make a pass at me, just to prove to myself that I could say no to him and mean it, without hating myself.

Duane was talking to someone about his cold, complaining that he was too sick to go out for a few days. He wrote something on the back of a credit card slip, hung up and suggested that we go get some food. "Let's go to that place upstairs where you work, that nice place? Get a nice steak for lunch? How's that sound?"

No way. Not in the middle of the day. What if we ran into my mother, what if he recognized her from the western-wear store, and he started going on as if he was going to be her new son-in-law? Even when I denied it, it would be hell to explain and would trigger too many questions that I didn't want to deal with.

"No, I have to work in that place. I don't want to be hanging out there on my day off -" I bit my lip, but it was too late, it was already out.

He brightened a little. "You don't have to work tonight?"

"No." I wished I could disappear.

"Well, that's great! Now we can finally have that nice dinner together. Where d' you want t' eat lunch?"

"I don't know, I'm not hungry right now."

"That's okay, I'm not hungry either. We'll just wait. Meantime, I need for you t' take me to the drug store so I can get somethin' for my throat. Can you do that for me?"

"Sure." I dug in my purse for my keys. "Ready?"

"Uh, okay. Lemme get my shoes on and I'll be right there."

Yeah, fine. He moved very slowly, as if every movement was painful, making little soft groans as if he was fighting to keep his misery hidden from me. Once he had his shoes on, he had to examine every item on the nightstand, decide if it should stay there or go with him. I slung my purse over my shoulder and rattled my keys, trying to move him along, but he was not ready until he had lit another cigarette. Now, with him standing up and ready to go, it was safe to use the bathroom.

The fact that I already had a momentous headache before going outside prepared me for the nearly-noon sunlight. Holding my sunglasses tight against my eyes, I looked down at my feet as we walked down the stairs to my car. I drove to the drug store and tried to wait in the car, but he whined so hard that I gave up and went inside with him.

He had to look at every different remedy they had, picking up boxes of syrups, tablets, lozenges and comparing them to each other. "What exactly are you looking for?" I asked, impatient. I wanted to get us out of there before we ran into someone.

"Somethin' for my head and for my throat."

"So just pick something!"

"I'm tryin'! Which one of these d' you think?"

"I don't know, aren't they all the same?"

"I don't know, that's why I ask. I think I better ask someone who does know, huh?" He took an armload of little boxes and packages to the prescription counter and asked to talk to the pharmacist.

I wasn't sure if he was being serious or sarcastic. It occurred to me that the pharmacist, a white-haired man with glasses, was someone who worked and presumably lived in Wattlesburg, but was unknown to me. I marveled at how many people I had encountered around here during this little adventure with Duane who fell into this category: the waitresses at Selma's Waffles, minimart clerks, people at almost every public place I'd been with him. I'd never noticed that before. For such a small town, a place I had lived all my life, shouldn't I know more people? Look at how little I'd known about my brother. It was if I had been wandering around blindfolded in my own head for seventeen years. Maybe I was more invisible than I realized. Maybe no one knew who I was, either. Then and there, it was something for which to be grateful, but it gave me a strange and incomplete feeling.

He was trying to get the pharmacist to commit to one product or another, so I took advantage of his attention lapse and wandered over to the makeup. I was almost out of mascara. Absently fingering the eyeshadows, I jumped when Duane snuck up behind me.

"You don't need that junk. I don't know why pretty girls think they need all that crap."

There was that sharp edge again. I saw no need to test the point, I just wanted to get out of there. Back at the motel, I tried to drop him off alone at his room, but he insisted that I come upstairs with him and paint his throat.

"Do *what?*"

"Paint my throat. I got this stuff I use when my throat hurts and I need you t' put it in for me."

"You don't need me for that." My accelerator foot was itching to fly away.

"Yes I do! I can't do it myself, I won't get it where it needs to go."

God. "Just put your head back and dump it in. How hard can it be?"

"No! You gotta come and do it for me. Come on."

Too tired to fight him, I pulled the parking brake and jerked the keys out of the ignition. Just this one thing, and then I was gone. *What a baby.* I hated him and I hated myself. Going up the motel stairs in the wide open daylight, I was exposed and conspicuous under the bright, omniscient sky.

He rooted through a kit bag, handed me a small bottle that looked as if it came from an antique store and sat down on the edge of the bed, waiting for me to minister.

"If you already had this, why did we have to go to the drug store?"

"Cause I needed this stuff, too." He held up his little white paper bag, waited with his hands folded while I read the instructions on the ancient bottle.

"Okay, put your head back and open your mouth." I was poised with an eyedropper full of dark purple liquid, like a nurse with a thermometer.

"*Ahhgg,*" he gurgled distastefully as I squirted the stuff in his mouth, then gagged violently and fell over on his side as if I had shot him instead of medicating him, trying to cough it out. He dragged himself dramatically to his feet and stumbled to the bathroom to spit it out, gagging all the way. When he was finished, he came back and sat down again, announcing he was ready for more.

"What good's it gonna do if you just spit it out?"

"I won't spit it out."

"You just did! You acted like I poisoned you or something!"

"No, I just wasn't expectin' it t' taste that bad, that's all. I'm ready for it now."

"Fine." I measured out another dropper full. "Put your head back."

Obedient, he opened his mouth, head tilted back like a hungry baby bird. I squirted in as much as I could before he gagged again and doubled over, coughing so hard I was afraid he would vomit right on my feet.

"No more," he croaked painful through his painful coughing.

"Says here you're supposed to get two droppers full. You still got some left."

"That's enough. I don't want no more."

"Fine." I capped the bottle and set in on the night stand.

He stopped choking and looked at me, disappointed. "You're 'sposed t' take a firm hand with me. If I'm 'sposed t' have more, you gotta make me take it!"

"I'm not gonna make you do anything! You're just gonna spit it out and bitch about how bad it tastes, why should I bother?"

"I didn't spit it out the second time. I can't help bitchin,' I'm just a cranky old man. It's your job t' kick me in the ass and make me get better. It's my job t' be cranky and give you a hard time about it."

"Fine. Open up." He obeyed. I filled the dropper with as much as it would hold and emptied the whole thing down his throat in one forcible squeeze. "There. You're done."

He went through his gagging gyrations one more time, making exaggerated faces like a spoiled little boy gagging on spinach. "Boy, that stuff's *foul*," he rasped when he recovered what was left of his shredded voice.

"I thought you said you used this stuff before."

"Once, a long time ago when I had strep throat. I forgot how bad it tastes."

"That's the only other time you ever had a sore throat?"

"Pretty much."

With all that he smoked and the unhealthy way he lived, I found that hard to believe. Almost on cue, he lit another cigarette and went into another coughing fit.

"Gotta kill the taste somehow," he said, reading my thought. He coughed long and leisurely, bent over his cigarette with his elbows leaning on his knees. He looked like he wished for a beer. "Let's go on downstairs," he said when the cough subsided, standing up and putting his cigarettes in his shirt pocket. "I gotta do some work on the rig."

"Oh, are you gonna be leaving soon?" Did that sound casual?

"Not right away. I already called dispatch and told 'em I'm too sick t' go out for a couple days. Come on." He headed for the door.

"No, I gotta go home."

"Home? I'm just gonna do a little tinkering, it won't take long. You can sit and talk t' me while I work."

"I gotta go home. I got chores and stuff to do and if I don't see my parents sometime, they'll think I ran away again." *Oops,* dammit. I bit my lip, bit my tongue.

He didn't seem to catch my unintended disclosure. "Yeah, you're right. I almost forgot we ain't even married yet and you still gotta do what your mama and daddy say."

I let that one go by, preferring to take advantage of the opportunity to escape. Later, when I was away from there, I could be indignant about the implications of his remark.

"I'll see you later then, for dinner. Just come on by whenever you want."

"Well -"

"Please," he whined, sensing that I was trying to back out. "You been so good t' me, I just wanna take you out for a nice dinner, that's all. That's all."

I was unsure, looking around the room, trying to think of an excuse that wouldn't spark an unpleasant scene and more whining.

"Just a little dinner? I swear I'll be a good boy. Come on, you promised you'd have dinner with me."

"Fine. Dinner. Goodbye."

He smiled as I walked out. "Just come on by whenever you want," he called after me. "Wait, I'll walk you down."

I almost had the door closed before he said it. If I had been just a little faster, I could have pretended I didn't hear him. And he probably would have chased me until I had no choice but to hear him. He walked beside me without touching me and stared ahead, coughing as he went. For some reason, I felt sorry for him all over again, and uncomfortable with him and myself.

"I'm lookin' forward t' seein' you again," he said formally at the car, with a sad look that looked as if he knew it was a lost cause. "Sure beats eatin' alone, havin' someone nice t' talk to instead of sittin' all by myself and tryin' t' make up things in my own head t' keep myself company, people starin' at me and feelin' sorry for me 'cause I'm sittin' all alone. Sure makes a difference, y' know?"

"Yeah," I said uncertainly, not wanting to sound as if I knew first hand, but what else could I say to such a dismal picture? If I shunned him now, would I be repaid later by having to live out the same dismal picture myself?

"See you later, then."

"Bye," I said quickly, getting in the car and driving away before he could say any more, exhilarated at being free of him until dinner.

NINETEEN

My father was there when I get home, watching TV in the living room and drinking beer. Three empty beer bottles sat on the coffee table, next to a fourth, two-thirds full. In his hand was a fifth bottle, just about empty, tipping about sixty degrees to the right. The neat line of empties reminded me of Duane, an unwelcome similarity that made me shiver. No girl wants to marry a man like her father.

"Hey, Dad," I said to him on my way to the kitchen, without waiting for an acknowledgement. Finding a pot of leftover rice in the fridge, I dished myself a bowlful and poured a glass of milk. Taking the cold food back to the living room, I sat in the other chair, opposite my father.

"No work today, Dad?"

"Nah," he slurred. "I'm 'sposed t' do Walt Emmerson's lawn on Wednesdays, but when I get there, his bitch ol' lady says she got someone else to do it. Cocksucker can't even tell me himself," he said, forgetting he was talking to his daughter. "Has t' have his *bitch* tell me."

His words ran together and I bet if I looked, I would find a bottle of Scotch close by. "Cocksucker," he muttered to himself, taking the last swig from the beer in his hand. "Hate people can't tell you shit t' yer face, gotta have his bitch tell me. Know what I mean, baby?"

"Yep," I said through a mouthful of cold rice, trying to look like I was concentrating on the TV. Hoping if he saw I wasn't listening, he would shut up.

"Lookit that," he said, pointing at the TV with his beer bottle. "There's that fuckin' go-see-Cal. Can't get away from that asshole."

"Um-hmm."

"Think I should start dressin' like that?"

"No."

"Well, your mother does. She thinks he's so goddamn good-looking. Even if I did wear that cowboy shit like that, she'll still think he's better'n me." He sunk back in his chair, exhausted from his tirade, pulled a pint bottle from under the chair cushion. *I knew it.*

He unscrewed the cap and took such a long pull that I thought I would be sick, watching him. He slipped the bottle inside his shirt, next to his heart. Forgetting we were alone in the house, he was trying to whisper. "You think yer mother's havin' an affair?"

"No I don't, Dad, and I'm not gonna spy on her for you, so quit asking me."

"Yeah, yeah, I know." He pouted and fell back in his chair, as if he was expecting to have his mouth slapped for mouthing off at his mother, not his daughter. "You're gettin' t' be as mean as yer mother. I wasn't gonna ask you t' do nuthin' like that and I'm tired of you talkin' back t' me like that."

Sighing, I rolled my eyes, pushing chunks of rice around the bowl with my fork. I wished I had forsaken the food and come in through my bedroom window. "She's not having an affair with anyone."

"Not with Cal there, I mean *hell*, he's way down in L.A. Whaddaya think - Henry Montoya, he kinda looks like Cal there, eh?"

"No."

"Prob'ly even lets her call 'im Cal, don'tcha think? Huh?" He laughed obscenely, washing it back with the other beer and giggling into the bottle.

"Come on, Dad, she's not having an affair with anyone, she loves you." Even I didn't believe that, I didn't think she loved anyone anymore, but I couldn't imagine her having an affair, either.

He snorted at my insistence. "She don't love me, she ain't loved me since Steve died, she thinks I killed him." He started to cry, draining his beer to fuel his tears.

Knowing there was no answer I could give him, I picked up my milk glass and stood. "It's okay, Dad, she doesn't really think that." I left him there, crying and clutching the empty beer bottle, dropped my dishes in the sink and went to bed.

Having found out that Duane didn't like makeup, I piled it on for our dinner date. *It's not a date, I am not **dating** him.* The heavy makeup made me look ridiculously fake and I was sure it would get a negative reaction from him. I put on baggy jeans and a long red T-shirt that made me look frumpy and completed the look by leaving my hair uncurled. The whole effect was of a comic-book face on a housewife body. My reflection in the mirror looked, I hope, like someone no one would want to marry. Too boring, too unappealing, sexless, dumpy frumpy and lumpy... perfect.

My discontented dad was snoring in the living room, so I tiptoed out the front door. My mom pulled up as I was pulling out, giving me a confused look. I gave her a breezy wave and sped away before she could gesture for me to come back. Even if it was dinner with Duane, I was glad to be out of the house. One less evening at home was well spent, wherever I went.

At the motel, I sat in the car for a few minutes to steel myself. It would be fine, I told myself. My mother was already safe at home, Lula couldn't be far behind. Had to be, better be. *What time is it?* Six-thirty. Another fifteen minutes, just to be sure.

He opened the door before I had a chance to knock. He had showered and shaved, his wet hair was combed back and he was wearing a clean, but wrinkled flannel shirt. Although he seemed glad to see me, his greeting was a bit more reserved than usual and he still looked painfully ill. He made no comment about my makeup or appearance, just stepped outside and closed the door behind him.

"Thanks for comin' down," he said as he lit a cigarette, as if he had asked me over to sell him something.

I didn't know what to say - *you're welcome?* Whatever I had left to say was dwindling fast, so I said nothing. There was still dinner to get through. I felt less comfortable in his company every time I was with him - not because of anything he might do to me, I thought we were beyond that, but because of how uncomfortable I was with myself. Soon, I knew I would have to put a stop to this, before expectations got any further out of hand.

"Let's go over t' that place upstairs where you work? I know you work there and all, but it won't be like eatin' at the burger place, huh?"

"Fine." Whatever was easiest. Trying to think of another place was more effort than I had energy for. It must be safe by now. "Uh, I don't know though - I'm not really dressed for it."

"Oh, you're just fine. You look pretty as always."

Amazing. Now I was sorry I dressed like this, he didn't even notice the makeup. There was no predicting this guy.

In the lobby of the Restola, I put him between me and the burger job, looking at my feet as we passed by. Upstairs in the steakhouse, the hostess who greeted us was Gloria Brenner, who I'd known in school. One year older than me, she was not beautiful or popular, but she had connections into those circles built on gossip-feeds, and was always on the prowl for flaws and missteps to exploit to give herself ground. People like her were why I tried to pass through school invisible. The heavy makeup and frumpy clothes were a poor disguise and now, facing Gloria's evil eye, I couldn't remember what my point was supposed to be. We'd had one class together, an art class my last full year in school. Maybe she wouldn't remember me.

"Hey, Pattie!" Gloria greeted me with fake warmth, looking me up and down. "I haven't seen you for a long time. I heard about your br -" Gloria stopped herself just in time, and I realized I was shaking my head and pleading with wide eyes for her to shut up. Then I realized I looked like I could be pregnant in my frumpy outfit. Gloria looked at Duane, looked at me and I could see her come to that very conclusion. She would tell others.

"Hey Gloria, I didn't know you worked here." I wanted to disappear.

"Yeah! I just started last week," she said, leading us to a table. "I was going to Fresno State, but I just got back. I might go to J.C. in Bakersfield next semester."

"Oh." I did not want to encourage this conversation.

"Well," she said brightly, taking another long look at Duane and seating us in a candlelit booth. "You two have a nice dinner." She handed us menus and left with a smirk on her face.

"How come you didn't introduce me to your friend?" he said in a hurt voice.

"Because she's not my friend."

"She sure acted like she knew you."

"She's just someone I knew at school. She's not my friend, she's just one more person I was hoping I would never see again when I dropped out."

"Oh. I can understand that. I thought maybe you were ashamed of me."

"No." I hated his unnerving ability to hit right on what I was thinking. It was becoming more difficult not to sound irritated with everything he said. He had to know what I thought of him by now, the way he could read my mind. How could he believe I would marry him? What was so hard about saying, *Duane, I don't want to see you anymore,* and making it stick? I'd seen them do it on TV, they just *said* it. All of the advice columns and self-help articles I read said I could do that, but I was still afraid of sending him away with a negative opinion of me. I quashed all of this by burying myself in the menu. *New York Steak, fourteen ounce cut, steak and prawns, ten ounces of USDA Prime with six succulent jumbo prawns, breaded and deep-fried to perfection....*

"I know, I'm just fishin' for compliments is all," he said, ignoring my barrier. I remained hidden and he tried to draw me out with self-ridicule. "I know it's an annoyin' habit, but hell, I gotta get 'em somehow." He tried to laugh, to lighten the mood. I emerged from my menu to give him a cursory chuckle and this made him feel better. The waitress came and he ordered a beer and a steak, medium rare. I ordered a turkey sandwich and a diet soda. The waitress nodded while writing everything down, then went away without looking at me.

"Don't you want one of them drinks, that half-and-half stuff you like?"

"I'm underage, remember? I can't order drinks."

"You should've asked me. I'll order it for you."

"No, I don't want one. I just want Pepsi."

"Okay, you're the boss."

I had to grit my teeth to keep from jumping up and screaming, *I'm not your boss!* I was no longer trying to uphold any kind of conversation. The burden was on him. We waited for our food in silence, punctuated by his sneezing, coughing, sniffling and excuse-mes. At last, the food arrived, and I could pretend I was too busy eating to talk.

He inspected his food, took a bite of steak and called the waitress back. "Can you take this back and heat it up some? It's just about stone cold."

"Yes sir, I'm sorry, sir," the waitress said and disappeared with his plate.

I was mortified. I had never seen anyone send back a meal before and it seemed like an insulting thing to do. I felt sorry for the waitress and afraid she would think I was just as rude. He was polite about it, but the way he said *stone cold* made it sound like a personal affront.

He sensed my embarrassment and tried to explain. "I eat out so much, I just think they should give it to you right. Especially for the price of a steak."

"Okay, I didn't say anything." I looked down, picked at my fries. As long as I didn't voice my thoughts, he couldn't claim to be reading them.

"I guess I'm just a rude old man, that's all. Why don't you marry me and change my ways?"

I flushed and he took it back. "I know, I promised I wouldn't say nuthin' 'bout that. I'm sorry, I won't say it no more."

Good, was my sour thought, as I took a bite from my sandwich. The waitress returned with his food, carrying the steaming plate with a hotpad. He thanked her and apologized for being so much trouble.

"No trouble at all, sir. Enjoy your meal," she tossed back as she hurried away. I admired her for her grace. When we were finished eating, he left a generous tip.

"I'd ask you t' see a movie or somethin'," he said on our way outside, "but I'm so goddamn tired I'd prob'ly just snore right through it and ruin it for you. Besides, it's time for you t' put more stuff in my throat again, so why don't we just go home, huh?"

He lit another cigarette when we were outside and I marveled at how he failed to see any connection between his malaise and his smoking. Back in his room, we repeated the same ritual with the throat-painting. He acted the same way he did earlier, as if he enjoyed the mommy/little boy roles he had worked out for us and this annoyed me even further. This was too confusing, figuring out if he wanted a wife, a mother, a boss, or a nurse.

"I'm just gonna go ahead and go t' sleep," he said when the gagging and complaining were over. "You go ahead and stay up as late as you want, watch TV or whatever."

"I can't stay here tonight. I have to go home."

"How come?" He was whining again.

"I can't! What'll my parents think?"

"Oh. Yeah," he said, defeated, and sat down on the bed, already resigned to my absence.

It was that easy. Why hadn't I thought of that last night? It was so simple, I should have seen it. I didn't think very well at four in the morning. I resolved to work on that. "Well, bye. I hope you feel better."

"Night, darlin'," he said sadly, stood and opened the door for me. "See you tomorrow."

I got out before he could press me for plans. I would deal with him tomorrow. *Right now, let's just get the hell out of here.*

TWENTY

When the phone rang the next morning, I knew it was him. At least he waited until a decent hour this time; I was already awake and reading a book. This was to avoid the morbid ramblings of my drunken father, who was still parked in the living room chair, yelling at the TV.

Duane's voice was deathly hoarse as he begged me to come over and minister to him. "I think I got a fever, too," he whined. "Can you bring a thermometer with you when you come?"

"Fine." I hung up. That was it. *This is it.* No more, no more, no more. I repeated it over and over, letting my anger build as I dressed, aiming for that sense of urgency that I needed to do this. I hadn't given him a single thought all morning until he called. Listening to him whine and beg like that, disturbing my peace, finally forced something into place. No more playing nursemaid, no more tiptoeing around his emotions, no more forced conversations, no more stumbling into talk of marriage. The word made me shudder and I slammed the closet door to express my disgust. It bounced back open, making me even angrier and giving me a chance to slam it again.

"Hey, where hell y' think yer goin'?" my dad shouted after me as I hurried out the front door. "Get yer ass *back* here!"

I ignored him because he didn't mean it, slammed the front door, holding the knob to be sure it stayed slammed shut. There was no speech-rehearsing on the way to the Restola, I would just say it. *That's it.* I was sick of this game I had let go on for too long, unable to explain why I was playing it in the first place. I suppose he had been slowly making me angry with his whining implications that he was the only one who had ever suffered and with his insane talk of marriage.

Would I falter? *This is it.* When I reached the motel, I didn't hesitate, I didn't brace myself. There was a nasty scene coming, and I took deep breaths on my way up the stairs. How would he react?

Would it make a difference? What if he flipped out, started crying, got angry? This couldn't go on. Remember, he'd hit his wife once. What if he accused me of leading him on? If I didn't want him, I should have said so up front. Yes, I should have. I had no justification for that. There was nothing I could accuse him of in return, except being delusional.

Duane answered the door in his undershorts, bending over to hide himself. Without saying a word, he turned and crawled back into bed, moaning and sniffling. He looked ghastly and I felt myself falter, feeling sorry for him again. I closed the door after myself, picked up the medicine bottle and sat on the edge of the bed. He opened his mouth for the medicine without being told and took it without gagging.

"Did you bring a thermometer?" he croaked, licking his lips and puckering at the taste.

"No, I forgot."

"That's okay, I know I got a fever, only question is how much. Here, feel." He grabbed my hand and put it on his sweaty forehead.

"Yeah, feels like it." I pulled my hand away, wiping it on my thigh.

"I'm sorry I'm so sick, darlin'. Some kinda husband I'll make."

At the word *husband,* I took a deep breath, steeled myself for what was coming, edged away from him. "Duane, I'm not gonna marry you. Not now, not ever. I'm sorry."

He stared at me for a second, his expression blank, digested my announcement. He turned over on his side, with his back to me. "That's your business."

Stunned at his non-reaction, I repeated, "I'm sorry."

"That's your business," he repeated back, without facing me.

I stood up for a second, still expecting some kind of outburst, but he said nothing more. Feeling strangely disappointed, I left him there, alone and ill, to minister to himself.

Elated at my escape but at the same time, ashamed of something intangible, I drove straight to Elvia's house. If I went home, Duane would be calling, trying to get me to come back. I didn't believe for a second that this was the end of it. He had my phone number, he knew where I worked. The phone number I would change right away. Work, I would deal with. He would be back. I was lucky to have gotten out of the motel with a minimum of ugliness, but what if it was only temporary? Apprehension overcame my elation and there was a budding new self-hatred: *did I just destroy someone?*

If he came back, when he came back, the more obnoxious he was, the more he justified my action. But what if he wasn't obnoxious, what if he was just pitiful?

When I reached Elvia's house, it felt like I hadn't been there in months. Almost as if I hadn't been home in months. I checked behind me one last time to be sure there was no big rig roaring down the street after me, then ran to the front door.

"Where the hell have you been!" Elvia shrieked when she opened the door. "I've been calling you for *days.*"

"Nowhere." As non-committal as possible, shrugging my shoulders. "I been really tired lately. I haven't felt good, either."

"Your dad said you weren't home."

"When?"

"Yesterday. Today."

"Well, I'm not home today 'cause I was on my way over here. I was home yesterday, but I was asleep. My dad doesn't know what planet he's on, much less who's on it with him. He still thinks my mother's screwing Cal Worthington."

"Yeah." Elvia laughed, accepting and dismissing my explanation with one word and at that moment, my life returned to its normal, directionless track.

I am him, he is me
ill and abandoned in that empty motel bed
entire body rigid a long time after the door slams
my head pounds my gut churns until I am rendered numb
sealed off for good by that door slam
I thought I found salvation but it wasn't for me
The walls close in, they're squeezing my brain
I have to go
there's a joke in here somewhere, I just can't think of it
What is meant for me? Salvation, like everything, has a price
and I have nothing to offer in return
nor do I have the tools to build my own
These last days were my happiest and my saddest

while I have ignored what was stupidly clear
It's clear now

Today the eternal pain in my head is king of all my demons
immediate and ever present
other lesser demons can be suppressed
temporarily
but this one never leaves me, pounding away at my skull as with an ax
the ferocity of its attack is beginning to tell
I can almost feel my skull cracking open
then it will feast on my brains, yum yum yum
Get up, get dressed, take more cold pills and light a cigarette
lifebreath
first draw makes me lightheaded, sits me down on the bed
keep sucking on the smoke, resist the urge to lie down
lest I not get up again
a prolonged coughing fit leaves me gasping for breath
and clutching my burning chest
there is no liquor in the room
I will take care of that on my way out

pull on socks and boots, stand and give myself another headrush
pause for another cough, this one not so bad
light another cigarette and walk down
leave the matching shirts on the dresser
leave all but my wallet, my jacket and keys
Breathe the fresh air through my cigarette while the cold sun feeds my headache
head and heart pound in unison, can't catch my wheezing breath
Get my twelvepack, my Red label and my two packs of cigarettes
drain the first beer in the parking lot it feels so good on my throat
for a moment, my gorge rises, will it back down
hold my stomach, my breath and my beer with the same hand
with one long grateful belch, I can continue on
climb up and lock myself in the rig, my last and only home
liquor rides with honor on the passenger seat
A familiar world returns
the welcome way the seat fits my backside
the singular way the windshield frames the world
It's mine alone
The engine begins its warmup and I prepare for the road

wallet on the dash, logbook in the sleeper
unwrap a fresh pack of lifebreath, open a fresh beer
then the scotch
breath in the rich heady fumes, real good whiskey such a rare treat
I should have treated myself more often
Ahh, one generous drink, one more, put it away for later
chase it with the cold beer, suck my smoke while the engine warms
The headpounding defies the alcohol, taunts me with its mastery
I will be with you always always always
in the glovebox are painpills left from the broken leg
I will save them for later

pull my rig out of the parking lot and don't look back
once on the freeway, take another drink of scotch
put it away until I get there, medicate my tortured head with the beer
The weather is cloudy and it's drizzling when I reach highway 41
but like most California rains it doesn't last more than a few miles
No radio, sometimes I prefer the pure sounds of the road
there's a certain peace to be heard
wind hums, tires hum, punctuated by other vehicles passed and passing
looking for that near-painless trance
induced by the engine hum and the dotted white lines
deepening twilight blankets the highway sights and narrows my vision
reduces the world to its purest form:
a narrow tapering black and white ribbon
framed by a windshield and a pair of headlights

it's fully dark by Pismo Beach
roll down the windows to smell the sea air blowing biting cold
and sending my lungs into spasms that bend me over the wheel
rips out of my chest like knives
Great stuff, I say to the breeze, roll up the windows
before my smoky air can escape
A three-quarter moon lights the pastel-tinted postcard town
When I see the ocean, I park, kill the engine
collect my bag of whiskey, beer and cigarettes
don't forget the painpills, this is the later I was saving them for
take two, wash down with the whiskey, climb down with my goodies
The cold ocean wind is bonechilling, the road is deserted
wind ripples through the cypress tree guardians lining the road

beer cans clatter and shift in the bag as I limp through the trees to the beach
I must be in a campground, suddenly in the midst of sleeping RVs
tucked in beside weathered picnic tables
What happened to the ocean? then my feet are on sand
and I'm staggering as if drunk
I can hear it but I can't see it
stumble forward, follow the roar of the waves to the top of a dune
There.
The ocean, where one world ends and another begins
lose my footing going down the dune
alarming stab of pain when the broken leg buckles beneath me
clutch my bag until I stop sliding
drag my painful self to my feet and struggle across the sand, closer to the water
drop my bag on the sand and drop my aching coughing wheezing body
next to the bag
open a new beer and drink, set it in the sand
find the whiskey and drink, set it next to the beer
light a cigarette and draw, set it on end next to the hootch
Monuments.
Empty the vicodins in my hand, count seven
swallow all seven with the whiskey, then the beer, then the cigarette
the cigarette has a pleasant grainy-saltiness from the sand
and I roll the grains around the roof of my mouth as I smoke
Already I feel better, water always does that for me
this isn't just any water, this is the Ocean
this very water here in front of me spreads all the way across the world
reaches unimaginable depths, touches unimaginable places
the god of all waters, this ocean, Pacific peace
whose waves speak only to me
whose words only I understand
whose pain only I know
where one world ends and another begins

the wind picks up, carries the finer grains of sand with the seaspray
moonlight-sparkling waters roll and throw their shadows back at the moon
who darts in and out of the fast-moving clouds
The surf surges and crashes as though the very hand of God
pounds for my attention
where are the rewards where is my heaven, the promises made to my ancestors
the satience of the forest lands and the prairies and the drowning of the waters

light another cigarette and the reward is another coughing siege
that leaves me on my side gasping for breath
as soon as I can breathe I'm coughing again, gagging, near to throwing up
pour more whiskey down my throat but the fire refuses to be doused
open another beer, now warm
and that's still better than a poke in the eye with a sharp stick
The coughing and the pounding in my head are drowning out the voice of God
in the surf
I have to hear what He's saying I have to quiet my head get closer to the water
the sand under my shaky feet moves like quicksand
I struggle to stand, wave my arms for balance, like one of those dancing
treeshadows
I have already passed through the gate
now I belong to the seashore
now I am one of those twisted wind-dwarfed trees
posted on the dune by the ocean
waving my green arms to God's choir singing from the waters
and skipping on the epiphanic wind
The dizziness stabilizes
I walk to the edge
arms outstretched to the waves
the pounding surf-song finally overcomes the pounding in my head
instead of a shock, the cold water is a comfort
cools my fevered limbs as with the cooling hand of Jesus
throw off my heavy jacket and walk in
let the water embrace me
gather me to the breast of God
wash me away to salvation

In time, the apprehension wore off and I stopped expecting him to pop out at every turn, but there was still something about it that I couldn't shake off. I still had dreams. If it was a dream, I might not shake it for the rest of my life. If it wasn't a dream, it will be mine for millenniums of lifetimes. I never told anyone about him. How could I explain to anyone else what I can't explain to myself? There is no explanation of which I can be proud. Elvia above all would not understand. She would ask the same question I ask myself: *why would you bother?* and there is no answer to that except to see that there were no winners in a game that was played in the lives of two people, where the prize is to be forever plagued by the question, *what happened here?* and then to have it engraved on your tombstone, *what happened here,* the best that could ever be said of your life.